Tales of Forever and Now

Xandra Noel

Copyright © 2022 Xandra Noel
Cover design - mageonduty
All rights reserved.
ISBN: 9798409390068

This is a work of fiction. References to real people, locations, events, organizations or establishments are intended for the sole purpose to provide authenticity and are used fictitiously. But, if you do happen to walk into a forest and find a fae prince, you need to message me immediately!

Tales of Forever and Now

-Tales of Earth and Leaves book 2.5-

Xandra Noel

Follow your heart ♡

To Rhylan

Who somehow managed to get his own book

"And that's how I got to meet Beyoncé! I was escorted through a corridor full of curtains and doors, each member with an Oscar under their belt. You name the actor, I guess they were there. My legs were shaking too hard and I couldn't focus on what was in front of me. As we reached the main door, her name appeared displayed in huge lettering, like one of those retro Hollywood signs. When we knocked on it, freaking Beyoncé greeted us with a smile. I had a chat with her for about five minutes and even got a hug!"

"Top 5 moments of my life? You know it!

And that is all for today. I will upload footage from the premiere in the next video. Till then, stay happy and wear that smile!"

As soon as I ended the vlog I released a slow breath and took a few seconds to unhook the smile everyone loved so much, while I wondered if I would ever be able to post a photo of just me. Randomly posing in a mirror, without makeup, having just woken up after a troubled night. Probably not.

I loved social media and I adored my life. I lived for these events and for meeting new people. I adored chatting away with the likes of Brad Pitt or Beyoncé as though I was one of them, when in reality all I did was plaster my face across the internet and hope for the best. Sometimes, in moments like these, while waiting for my sister to come back from her trip where she was doing something meaningful, I felt that life had more to offer.

Anwen changed so much in the past two years and what I admired most about her was that even though her heart had been shattered over and over, she still managed to find meaning. I, on the other hand, felt empty. I did not know how much longer I could do this job. How long until they replaced me for a younger, more beautiful woman they would all decide to follow one day and all the love and millions of followers would vanish like a lipstick stain from a satin blouse.

Luckily, the sound of an open door, which I surprisingly managed to hear over the music I blasted out in my friend's room, took me out of the misery of these recurring thoughts and Anwen walked in, looking a lot more elegant than I expected her to.

"Bestie!" I snickered and her face lit up, making her drop the fancy shoes she carried in her hand as she jumped to hug me. Tighter than usual. Was there something wrong?

"What are you doing here?" My friend asked with a glance of surprise. Whatever happened, it was obvious that she needed me.

"I have a few days off and your mom said you were coming back tonight, so I popped in for a sleepover," I offered her my wide vlog-smile which seemed to relax her enough to release me from the tight embrace. I kept to myself the fact that I had nothing and no one waiting for me at my apartment, so I craved her company as well.

Anwen sat next to me and took a deep breath. One of the many things we had in common. We both had to settle ourselves before making a big announcement. So I prepared myself for whatever it was she wanted to share.

"I brought a man home," she uttered quickly, then stopped to scan me up and down and the reaction her words would draw from me.

OK... Anwen brought a man home. Let's start with the obvious. "Who is he?" I asked.

"It's complicated, and I need you to help me get rid of him without being too obvious, because I need him back in exactly forty-three and a half days."

"Right," I laughed again and pulled the pillows back to make myself more comfortable, grabbed the laptop and started playing music again. I liked to play it as loud as possible, loud enough to cover everything, even my own thoughts.

"I'm serious!" My sister protested, but I ignored her with a simple "Aha" and checked the upload time of the vlog I just finished editing. I knew Anwen too well to fall for these kinds of jokes and I didn't really understand why she would start mocking me like this all of a sudden. Let it be her way. We all deal with stress the best we can.

"As you wish, just remember my words when we go down for dinner," she approached me long enough to shout the words into my ear then headed to the bathroom, from where, a few minutes later, she came out in a casual outfit and a messy wet bun, proving my theory. Not a single woman would go down to dinner dressed like that, if she truly brought a man home. Especially with how picky the Odstars were on formal occasions.

"Ready for dinner?" She shoved her head over the laptop screen to check my scheduled releases; she loved watching my vids before anyone else. When I first started this, Anwen had been the one to help me edit and share her ideas; we even helped each other with ring lights and Instagram photos.

"Let's go," I replied and hurried from the bed. My stomach grumbled, so I made my way first through the doors and led Anwen through her own house. Truthfully, I had spent so much time here since my parents passed, I knew every single room and corridor there was, I had my own password for the alarm system and sets of keys, so in some ways, this felt more like my house than my apartment. And the best part was that there were always people here.

When Anwen and I reached the dining room hallway, I heard another man's voice talking to Jason. Which I found odd because I hadn't been instructed for any company, so I pushed the doors open and made my way into the dining hall. Where I indeed found Jason and a tall man, silhouetted by the bar, each holding a glass. I immediately spotted the bottle and realised the importance of this visit. Jason had popped open an old Hennessy, so he clearly wanted to impress the guest who stood nonchalantly by his side and chatted away as though he had known Jason all his life.

When Anwen's father spotted us, he turned and made his way to greet his daughter, making the guest turn. Only to show the reflection of the most beautiful man I had ever seen.

Dressed in black from head to toe and freakishly tall, his dark hair arranged in a trendy do and those eyes. Penetrating into my very soul, their darkness so bleak I wanted to dive into it and be surrounded by his gaze.

I froze; the only words coming out of my mouth were so low that I doubted even my friend heard them. "You brought a man home," the air in my lungs cut out after every word.

"No kidding," Anwen huffed at me, upset that I didn't believe her in the first place, and stepped towards her father to trap him in a hug.

For the first time in a long while, I did not know how to react or what to say. I was beyond happy for my friend and the fact that she managed to find this fine specimen, yet my heart started thumping like crazy and I barely contained my impulses while a fully developed porn movie played inside my mind, where that dark guy was the star. There was something about him, apart from being absolutely gorgeous, nothing like any model I'd ever seen. He looked like he had some kind of eternal beauty and seemed... dangerous somehow. Definitely hiding something.

"And who is this beautiful lady?"

His voice enveloped every pore in my body and made me shiver with goose bumps and desire. If I could breathe in sex, it would be his image and damn it, I'd make sure he gives me some pleasant dreams tonight. Images of my body interlocked with his in dangerous positions flashed out of my mind as I spotted him approaching.

"Cressida Thompson," Anwen responded on my behalf, while all I could do was admire the man and take in every detail of his perfect image. He truly was the embodiment of lust, and he knew it. With that extravagant look on his face and a dashing smile, he took yet another step closer to display his perfectly tailored designer clothes and a scent that overpowered every single one of my senses. I heard Anwen making a brief introduction, but the only thing my focus lingered on was his hand.

"I have no doubt that she is. Her beauty is beyond anything I've seen in recent history." As he spoke the words, his fingers reached for mine, our skin connecting to form an array of jolting sensations. And his lips. God damn it, his lips curving perfectly to reach my skin and place a kiss on my hand. Was it too early to faint? Because I was ready to fall into his arms.

"I don't believe we have been introduced," the only words I mustered while my eyes splayed themselves on him, feasting on this image of the man of my dreams. One that I hadn't even thought possible to exist, yet here he was, gathering my wildest desires in one stunning body.

"Rhylan Gordon, but you can call me Rhy. All my friends do." His voice sounded sensual. He too liked this, I realised. It was not only his voice that announced his intrigue, because the man kept caressing my hand as though he had just discovered some sort of treasure and did not want to let it go.

"There is no need for that. Cressi has too many friends as it is. Men friends," Anwen felt the need to slide herself in between us and announce this nonsense, which immediately woke me up. Was my friend jealous? Did I overstep? In her room, she had said she wanted to get rid of the guy. Maybe she was confused or joking? I turned to my friend and grimaced, and I immediately saw her eyes, signalling me to cool it down. Fine, I took a deep breath in. I'll just spend dinner gathering enough images of this man's body to last me for the next few nights. Mama still needed her fun.

An hour and a half into dinner, I found out that Rhylan had curiously met Anwen in Evigt and he was an investor that needed to go back to his country and take my friend with him on Autumn Solstice. A bit too horoscopey for my taste, but each to his own. He spoke eloquently; he behaved well; he took care of my friend's needs.

From my position at the table opposite them, next to the empty seat Erik used to occupy no less than two years ago, I took the time to watch him. Really watch him. He had some sort of connection with my sister, because he cared for her. More than she needed him to, almost to the point of babysitting her and anticipating some of her needs before she expressed them. He spoke to Elsa but all the while refilled Anwen's water, then turned to Jason and passed her another bun from the basket because she was two mouthfuls away from finishing the one she was currently biting into. What I did not understand was why? And why was Anwen so resigned to the idea of having him by her side, accepting him with such ease when she never even bothered to mention him to me?

"Why is your stay so exact, Rhy?" I smiled at him widely and fluttered my eyelashes the way TikTok taught me to, making him feel at ease and not at all under investigation.

"Autumn Solstice plays a part of utmost importance in my plans, though I am sure Anwen would like to tell you more herself once you two take some time to get reacquainted after dinner." He blinked slowly and offered me a smile that told me he was onto me and my not-so-subtle questions.

Rhylan's stare pierced through me for a few seconds and I'd never been more vulnerable. He had just undressed me with that gaze. As though he knew my deepest desire and could just splay it out at any second, along with my fears. He looked at me like he knew all the secrets of the universe and saw me for what I was. Not the influencer, not the dashing blonde model or the businesswoman behind my brand, but just me, Cressida, a lonely girl who lost her parents and had to replace the void with whomever had her.

I sighed and said goodbye to the platter of vegan cakes brought out especially for me and dropped my fork to draw the room's attention. "Anwen and I will retire for the evening, if you'll excuse us. It was a wonderful surprise to meet you, Rhy." I grinned at him, sharing a genuine smile, one that I hadn't displayed in a long time. "I can't wait for breakfast," I added and stood from my seat, urging Anwen to do the same.

We walked as silently as we could up the stairs, making sure not to disturb the dinner conversation as we headed back to her room. As soon as I closed the doors with Anwen inside, I unleashed the million questions that gnawed at me for the past two hours. Who is he? How come you brought him home? Are you two together? Where do you find men so hot? How come you didn't tell me about this? Is this something recent? I must have ranted for about a minute or two, throwing random questions at her without giving my friend a second to actually take the time to respond. I had to get it all out of my system until I quieted enough to allow an explanation.

Anwen's words found me settled on her mattress, in a comfortable yoga pose, hugging her favourite pillow, which I stole every time I spent the night.

"Is it my turn now?" She made an effort and waited until I relaxed enough to receive said explanation, to which I nodded multiple times. "I am eagerly awaiting," I replied, and waved my hands to give her the invisible spotlight.

My friend took a deep breath, like she wanted to announce some bad news before she started speaking. "For this to work, you will need to listen and not freak out. The only thing that is important right now is for you to know that Rhylan is not charming or good." She wanted to say more, but all the images and the dirty thoughts I had accumulated since I saw this man came rushing in.

"Is he bad? Bad boy Rhy?" I giggled in delight and started playing with my lower lip on a whim.

Anwen's eyes widened, and she panicked. "Cressi, no, it's not like that. You need to stay away from him," she tried using her business tone with me, to absolutely no avail. I was the one who instructed her on how to speak to people and command authority. Shame on her to try to use my own tricks against me.

"Why did you bring him home, then?" I frowned, becoming unaware of whatever she tried to explain. She had arrived with a stunningly charming man, who lived for her attention and looked to be a perfect gentleman, who was also a businessman and wanted to spend more time with my friend. Why the hell not?

Anwen started telling me about the plane ride and how she'd been blackmailed by Rhylan to bring him home and invite him to live in the house. Which made absolutely no sense. What need would he have to blackmail someone just to stay in their home?

As usual, my words did not keep a hold of themselves and I heard myself saying that I was in love with him and if my sister wouldn't have him, I would be delighted to. My breath caught with the confession and my heart started jolting because... part of it was true. I did not know how or why this man could affect me in such a way, though there I was, suddenly becoming a lost puppy craving cuddles.

"Cressi, stop! Anwen almost shouted at me and I froze for a second before I cuddled my friend with kindness. She looked scared and lonely, so I did my best to settle her. I knew she had lost so much and even though we didn't talk about it anymore, Ansgar had been a big part of that loss. Whatever happened in that forest, wherever he went, that man left cracks in an already broken heart.

"Cressi, there are so many things I kept from you, so many things you don't understand," she told me while trapping me into a tight hug that we both needed.

"Tell me, Anwen," I encouraged her. "Tell me what is happening to you. Make me understand and I promise I will help," I whispered. This was us, we had been through so much together and no matter what this new thing was, no matter what she told me, I would do my best to help and support my friend, just as we'd done since we were little girls.

Without even looking at me, a sudden determination overpowered my friend, who snatched my laptop and started typing frantically, only to place the screen in front of me and ask me to read an article. I was slightly annoyed and wanted to protest, but she begged me so I understood its importance.

While I read, footsteps stopped in front of the door and I distinctly heard Rhylan's voice wishing us a good night. My heartbeat spiked abruptly and before I had a chance to respond, Anwen ushered him away. He left quickly, not without leaving a giggle behind the doorway. One that curled into my chest and I knew it would accompany many thoughts afterwards.

Having no alternative, I read part of the article Anwen had shown to me, struggling to understand why she needed me to learn about a dark fae creature who lived in a place called Fire Kingdom and had unknown powers.

"Why are you showing me this?" I finally asked, bored with the Dungeons and Dragons kind of story the website invented.

"Because that's what he is!" Anwen explained, her face inundated with sudden relief, as though the fact that she could tell someone had released whatever burden she kept for only herself. "Rhylan is Fear Gorta, and you need to help me get rid of him."

"Anwen, what are you trying to tell me?" I settled in place enough to give myself time to scan my friend, giving her my full attention. Also, I wanted to make sure I heard her right, because this, whatever she was trying to tell me, did not make any sense at all.

"I know it sounds crazy," she tried to explain. Okay, at least we know that. Crazy people don't understand they are crazy, so at least we know Anwen hasn't suddenly decided to adopt a paranormal lifestyle.

"Remember all the research I did before going to Evigt? How Erik told me to go there, or at least, so I thought?"

Of course I remembered, my sister had been focused on the task for months, obsessing over her brother's last words, which did not make sense to either of us. For a while, I thought that Erik's sudden passing had taken a toll on her, as one would expect when her long life companion suddenly vanished from her future.

However, when we started doing research and we

discovered a forest with the same name Anwen swore had come out of her brother's lips, things pieced together. Especially since it was owned by the Swedish royal family and we all knew Jason's pride with regards to their friendship. Something must have been there, something that Erik needed her to find. And I supported her every step along the way, from reaching connections to helping her create a proposal for her family to allow it to happen.

She was now trying to explain that she found something in the forest, though not what we both expected, which sounded strange because every time we talked and I asked her about her findings, she always reported back with no news. Was she feeling guilty for moving on? For leaving whatever happened to Ansgar behind?

In the few months they'd been together, I had never seen my friend happier; she looked as radiant as a globe of light by his side, but when she returned without him, her chest became a bleak place, as if she had left her heart in Evigt.

"Just stay with me," Anwen raised her hands and extended her palms towards me, wanting to trap my thoughts and avoid me projecting them further on.

"Ansgar never told me he was a biologist. It is something he let me assume."

"He only said he came to the forest to care for the plants."

"Because that's what he was assigned to do."

"By the royal family of which he belonged."

"From the Earth Kingdom."

"Of the faeries," she finally took air into her lungs while my face changed from one emotion to another, forcing an array of thoughts to surge through my mind.

"As in... Ansgar is a faerie?" I barely breathed.

"He is a fae," my friend corrected.

"What's the difference?" I frowned. She told me about some characteristics of the fae and how they looked more like humans than the faeries, somehow all I could think about was the man she had brought home.

"And Rhy is this kind of fae. A Fear Gorta?" I wanted to clarify.

Anwen nodded quickly and gazed at me with part hope, part fear. Her eyes started filling up with tears, expecting me to have some sort of crisis, to be upset with her. I wanted to jump in and hug her, tell her that no matter what she went through, I would be there for her, yet at this point, it looked like she wanted to be understood and believed more than anything.

So I gathered all the information I had, everything she told me just then, and created the story as I understood it. I summarised her arrival in Evigt, meeting Ansgar, this

Rhylan's involvement and how she had suffered for an entire year, thinking her lover to be dead.

"So Ansgar is alive, in a faerie kingdom, where I am guessing you and Rhy will travel to on Autumn Solstice, which I assume is a big thing in the faerie world or something," I made sure to finish the sentence with a smile, because Anwen looked like she would burst into tears and check herself in a mental facility. She nodded eagerly, somehow afraid of my reaction. The thing that annoyed me the most was—

"I still don't understand why I can't fuck him," I contested with offence.

"Seriously?" Anwen's eyes widened to double their size after my statement, if such a thing was possible.

I sighed. "No, I get it. You go to a magical world and find yourself the sexiest guy ever, and then bring another one home for me. I like it." I smiled and licked my lips in delight, thoughts of Rhy popping to mind again.

"Are you not freaking out about this?" she asked with no small amount of surprise.

I huffed, pointing at the crazy things I witnessed at private parties, stuff that no one could ever think possible. Like vampire foreplay with actual blood, orgies on display or people believing themselves Illuminatis and sacrificing animals on an altar in front of their guests. One of the reasons I did not attend private parties any more, unless hosted by a friend or someone I trusted. As much as a famous person can be trusted. Either way, two sexy as fuck men calling themselves faeries was the least of my worries.

Anwen could not help herself any longer and jumped into my arms, making me fall underneath her weight, shedding tears which I had a feeling were more from relief than hurt. I hugged her as tightly as I could, for the longest time, until she settled enough to be able to have a proper chat.

We turned on the TV at high volume and found some dumb reality show to make it more believable and while Anwen excused herself in the bathroom; I called downstairs and asked for two bottles of champagne, because this conversation would be long and stressful, so we needed an energy boost.

When she returned, Anwen explained everything to me with details, how she met Ansgar, how they fell in love, how Rhylan attacked her and the tricks he played until getting what he wanted. A lot of things clicked with this new information, which gave me a much better understanding of everything my friend had been through, and I wanted to strangle myself for not putting two and two together and asking more questions until she finally told me what happened. The fact that she went through all this alone killed me and I swore to be by her side from then onwards.

"First, we need to check if Ansgar is truly alive," I started forming a plan, which I typed on my phone as I spoke. "And you need to get a copy of that contract. Then we rummage through his belongings and see what we can find. Every man has something incriminating, so it is a given that we find some weird shit in his room. We blackmail him into giving Ansgar back, job done," I smiled and put the phone away while chugging the rest of the champagne. The world started spinning and that's how I liked it most.

Anwen and I settled between the pillows, chatting away in the dark with the buzzing of the TV in the background and talked the world away. I loved being like this with her, just like old times when we did not understand loss and loneliness, when we were just two young girls with hopes and dreams, our biggest worries, that we did not know how to kiss a boy properly.

My friend's wavy hair settled over the pillow and left an orange scented aroma — she had become obsessed with this particular smell since she returned from Evigt and somehow, I knew it had to do with her losses. It's strange how we claw onto something that brings us closer to our loved ones. Or whatever image we are still able to hold of them.

That night, however, I had better plans with my sleep, with the comfort the image of a dark-haired, tall man had carved into my mind. I blinked a few times in the darkness, while settling comfortably inside the duvet, and thought about him. Alone in the next room.

And I wondered if even monsters need to feel loved.

Day 2

When my eyes opened, images of smoke and waves of darkness rippled around the sun that struggled to make its way through the heavy curtains. My head throbbed and I immediately started regretting finishing up that third bottle we snuck in from the kitchen. Almost.

I pushed Anwen's messy hair away from my pillow. During the night, she crawled to my side of the bed and we slept hugging one another, and opened my eyes enough to find my pink phone case. When I tapped the screen, an image of Anwen and me in Paris appeared along with the time. 14:03.

"Of course we missed breakfast," I sighed and shifted, making Anwen wake with a jolt. And fall back asleep in the next second.

I knew how much my friend hated waking up and how she needed an hour or two to be fully functional even after that, but this was not the time for pleasantries. We had a plan to execute, so, with little patience, I kicked her out of bed before I hurried into the bathroom to get ready.

"I just peed in front of him," were the words that awaited my return when I left the bathroom twenty minutes later, as I found Anwen eating a banana. I could not help a chuckle.

"You need to learn manners, my girl," I giggled and took possession of her vanity to display all my make-up selection and arrange my face. Another twenty minutes and I was happy with the outcome. My eye bags needed a bit of extra care; nothing an Instagram filter could not sort out and I tagged Anwen as well. Caption: *Anwen still recovering after a crazy night of champagne and plotting to conquer the world.*

I did not wait for the first likes to pop in, eventually they always did. Be it five million or twenty, I did not care any longer. It had become a job, something I grew accustomed to doing every single day and instead of checking for smiles and good times, I always criticised angles, hashtags and background lighting.

Before we even had a chance to go through the plans, Rhylan announced his presence at the door with a knock and a low sound that echoed very much like a clearing of his throat, no doubt to get our attention. And so he did, because as soon as she sensed him, Anwen hurried and pushed me towards the door, shoving me in the first line of the faerie blow while she ran back into the safety of blankets.

"Good morning," I opened the door with my best smile and displayed my boho golden dress that I knew did wonders for my boobs. Back straight, chest up, here we go.

"Good afternoon," he displayed a proud grin and those eyes, those amazing dark eyes, scanned me from head to toe, more than once. Were it not for the high heels that kept my knees under constant tension, I would have melted. Call me ice cream and give Rhy a big spoon.

"You look ravishing," he did not hesitate to state the obvious, his gaze struggling to find an appropriate point between my eyes and my breasts.

"And what do you normally do with a ravishing woman, Rhy?" If I were to play this game, I had to do it right, and might as well enjoy it, so I extended my hand to him. In my defence, he had already closed the distance between us and leaned against the doorframe. I allowed a finger to reach him and playfully scratch his biceps, leaving a trail on the black shirt.

"Whatever she asks me to," he replied with no small amount of nonchalance and, very confident in his right to do so, rested his hand on my hip. I hoped he could not sense the drumming of my heart, because it sounded like a full Ibiza July night up there.

First things first, mama, let's get him out of here. I controlled the insatiable pounding. "She is very hungry at the moment, and knows a place where they make the best avo burgers." I smiled like an innocent girl, showing how I needed a man to provide for me and bring me food. Even made sure to accidentally flutter my eyelashes a few times. And now for the big finale.

I shifted my hip and made sure to do it slow enough that his palm followed along, then changed my weight from one foot to another and tilted my head to make an A silhouette. With that dress, the tension in my calves, innocent eyes and a smile, I had to have him. "Good company is scarce around here—"

I blinked and waited. One second, two, three. *Bingo!*

Without saying another word, Rhylan took my hand and started pulling me after him down the stairs in a hurry, like he feared I would change my mind. Poor lamb, little did he know.

We passed through the halls and the main courtyard and I could not help but notice that he had gotten himself very acquainted with the house in just one morning. Someone's been busy while we slept.

It was only when we reached the parking lot that he spoke again.

"I—I don't have a car," he turned and towered over me. He must have been six foot five or taller, because even with the high heels, I barely reached his chin. The style, the elegance and those dark glances made the package complete.

I didn't let him invent an explanation. It would be futile, so I reached into my small purse and grabbed my keys, then placed them into his hand. "The red Maserati," I announced while I busied myself with my phone.

As always, the perfect gentleman, he opened the car door for me and asked me twice if I was sure I was alright with him driving, to which I nodded and kept myself busy, throwing him dashing glances. He always returned them.

Stroke his ego. Check.

I bet I could have him wrapped around my finger by the time we reached the restaurant.

I think I forgot my pink lipstick and we are already in the car. Can you check? I texted Anwen while asking the GPS to find our destination and within the next ten seconds, Rhylan started playing with big boy cars.

Prime time in NYC helped us get more acquainted during the car journey. Rhylan checked about three times that my seat belt was fastened, and struggled to divide his attention between me and the road ahead. From what I read on the laptop the day before, the type of faerie that he was did not allow him to die as easily as the others, so all the fuss and worry must have been for my benefit. For the frail mortal he had taken out of the house, for whose safety he felt responsible. I understood his choices. The last thing he needed was to accidentally damage me somehow and break whatever deal he had with my friend, so I kept the chat light. We talked about the weather, about food, he told me some traditions around the world and I pointed out a few buildings and played host.

By the time we reached the restaurant, the afternoon queue already started forming, so I knew it was time to exercise my smile. Rhylan opened the door for me and, after passing the keys to the valet, he turned towards the line. *Not today, baby, not while you're with me.*

"What are you doing?" I giggled in surprise, pulling him by the sleeve, and pointing at the entrance.

"There is a line," he looked at me, stupefied, as though he had never once in his life visited a restaurant. Had he?

"We don't have time to queue, plus I'm a regular here," I pointed out and displayed my runway walk across the entrance carpet and towards the doors, which magically opened for me while I was just a step away.

"Miss Thompson," I was greeted in and Rhy had no choice but to follow. "Table for two?" The man pointed his gaze to my companion and then back to me, while still managing to stare at my boobs.

"Please," I nodded and smiled again, then turned to Rhylan to make sure he followed as the server escorted us through the busy restaurant, with no available tables, and into the VIP section.

Once we were seated, we both thanked the host and within a minute, a bottle of red and two glasses appeared on the table, along with the menu and a section of on-the-house tapas.

I did not want to be ungrateful, so I fished out my phone, snapped a photo of my wine glass that gleamed in the light to display a rainbow on the crystal and tagged the venue.

When I pointed my gaze back at him, I noticed Rhylan watching me with newly acquired curiosity.

"You are—important," he pointed out the obvious. His raven eyes danced, like he wanted to catch every single detail I might exude during the conversation.

"And how do you feel about that?" I pierced him with a determined gaze as well, while I took a big sip of wine and pursed my lips to feel the rich taste.

"Intrigued," he admitted and somehow, within a split

second, reached across the table to find my hand.

I raised my brows without breaking eye contact. "Curious. Most men do not handle it too well," I admitted.

"I am not most men," Rhylan said as his fingers interlocked with mine, the touch of his skin sending goose bumps in places goose bumps should not be allowed in.

"You could say that again. I have never had a late lunch with a faerie," I smiled elegantly. *Time to have a chat, baby.*

His eyes widened in surprise for a mere moment, nevertheless, he did not let go of my hand, only tilted his head and scanned me again. Trying to read my next move.

"Apart from Anwen, I haven't had lunch with a human in over a century, so out of the two, I would say the honour is all yours," he displayed a dangerous smile.

By the time the appetisers arrived, both of us had removed our veil, and Rhylan pointed out how he enjoyed every single one of my hacks. "Hand on my chest and letting me drive were some nice tricks, I bet a lesser male would have already fallen at your feet," he continued to smirk while taking a big bite of his tapas platter, weirdly adding a bit of everything onto the olive oil dipped bread.

Do not worry, pretty boy, you will be too. Challenge accepted.

I tilted my head sweetly to the side and kept silent for a

few seconds, focusing on chewing my vegan bacon a bit too slowly and making a show of how tasty it was. Then, once I swallowed and licked my lips for a nanosecond, I turned my attention back to him.

"Tell me about yourself, Rhy. The real you," I asked, almost purring in delight.

He tensed a bit and no matter how much he wanted to push away the effect I had on him; the gesture made it more than obvious. He wanted me.

"What is it that you wish to know?" his voice came out rougher than I was used to.

"What the internet can't tell me. What Anwen doesn't want to see. I know there's more to you than sheer wickedness." I don't know why I admitted that, why I shared part of my beliefs when this was supposed to be solely a unilateral exchange, me pulling information, yet I enjoyed how his eyes sparkled at the mention of Anwen.

"Do you love her?" I asked again, giving no further explanation. We both knew who the subject of the question was.

He chuckled and his voice came out in ripples of darkness, then he pursed his lips and I had to take a few seconds to recover from the image and the way I almost sensed what those lips would do, were they to focus their attention some place else.

"Sometimes," he admitted with a sigh. "She is a strange person, but I will admit the downfall of our relationship culminated with me taking away her boy toy."

His features looked weirdly honest and a speck of light cropped in his eyes, as if he was enjoying the conversation and all the confessions he was able to make. Admissions he kept to himself until then.

"She's been through a lot, and you didn't help either, that's very true," I admitted and agreed with him so easily, like we were checking a shopping list.

"Is he really alive?" I asked, more in a whisper than an actual interrogation tone. I hadn't seen Ansgar many times, and it'd been on video only, though he seemed fairly shy and sweet. I did not know the prince or interacted with him for more than the few minutes when Anwen left him alone in front of the laptop, and even then, he panicked and did not really know how to address me or what to say. He was always polite and struggled to make pleasant conversation, though it was clear he had absolutely no idea what my occupation comprised.

What I could judge him on was the effect he had on my sister. A woman who arrived there broken and flourished in front of my eyes, deepening her smile with every visit he made. That was more than enough for me to like him, and to fight for him if I had to. Fight for them and their happiness.

"Did Anwen put you up to this? Is this some sort of interrogation?" he frowned and looked slightly disappointed that my interest in him hadn't been as genuine as he initially thought.

"Oh Rhy," I threw him an original Hollywood sigh, "you know the rules." I placed my finger on the rim of my wineglass and started moving it side to side, playing with the remains of the liquid pouring down back into the glass after I'd taken a sip. "Sisters before misters," I giggled, just as the server arrived with our mains.

He had ordered a juicy fillet mignon with caviar sauce and pickled radishes. Yuk. Mine was an avo burger.

"That doesn't look at all appetising," his eyes dropped from me to my plate, where the half an avo had fallen to the side, leaving a smudge over the fake meat.

I giggled. "It's an acquired taste. I hated avocados for the longest time and all of a sudden they are in trend and people learnt how to cook them. Now I eat them. Along with all the vegan wonders of this world," I put on my dreamy eyes. I loved technology and all the inventions and trends people came out with every day. Some made me question our intelligence, but avo burgers with a vegan chicken patty and garlic sauce? One of the wonders of the world!

"Is everything you do a statement?" he frowned while cutting into his tall steak.

"I have a short life, Rhy. Unlike you, I don't get to be here forever. So I do my part," I stated, making a point to escape a soft moan while taking a big bite of my food.

"And what is your part? Be dashing, charm every man in existence, accumulate wealth and skip queues using your tits?"

Was this bastard judging me? *Oh, game on, baby.*

"Actually, I have more money that I need in this lifetime, so every year I donate half of it to various organisations. This year, it so happens to be Anwen's foundation. Mommy and daddy left me a fortune, you know?" I winked at him and escaped a small whistle. God only knows how I did that. "As for my fancy lifestyle, I did absolutely nothing to earn that, apart from being in the right place at the right time. I started gaining followers while making YouTube videos about makeup and how blending brushes work and no, I will not say that I have some higher purpose than this."

Rhylan huffed. "You are the first human I heard in a long time to admit your uselessness and futile existence. It is refreshing, I must admit," he stopped to take another bite of his steak, fully aware of the blood boiling in my veins. "It's a good thing that you admit your limitations."

"My limitations? Excuse me, what are those? What does a centuries-old faerie man know about modern life?" Suddenly the food was stirring in my stomach, along with anger. A big pile of it.

"I have been here long enough to know that you are only looking to rip out benefits and give nothing back. If you do," he said while pointing at my food," you have to make a show of it and be seen. And judging by your profession," he stopped to stress the words and make sure I caught his mocking tone, "you live for attention and would be nothing without it."

What the actual fuck? I wanted to throw my drink in his face and leave, just drop the fucker with the check and go back home, to never see him again. I took a breath in. Anwen. This is what needed to be done. She needed time.

Okay, motherfucker, you want the hard truth? You want to know the modern world and take a stroll into fuckland? I'll take you.

"You are absolutely right. I did nothing to deserve this and I get attention everywhere I go. Which is why I can't even take out the trash anymore and had to buy an apartment at the top of the world, so drones can't fly over my house any longer. I can't go anywhere without taking an hour to arrange my face and look perfect and even then, I am having the same conversations, with the same people, being asked the same questions and I always have to be at my best and display a dashing smile. If a strand of hair is out of place, they will rip me apart. Because they love me," I added air quotes, making sure he was the one who understood my mocking tone this time.

"Exactly, which is why—"

"Oh no, pretty boy," I raised a finger in the air to silence him, "you had your chance to speak your mind. Now it's my turn." Strange delight came into his eyes, which widened just slightly at the way I cut him off. He settled and nodded, allowing me to continue.

"So yes, I will enjoy this lifestyle as long as I can. Because let me tell you, I am perfectly aware that as soon as I turn thirty or thirty-five, I will be forgotten. My body will start to age and I won't be seen as the sex bomb influencer I am now. Which I hate, by the way, but if that's the card I'm given to play, that's what I will do. Apart from a pretty face, a round ass, and a nice set of boobs, I don't have much else. And that's how the world sees me. It's the reality we live in. And I absolutely despise it, because let me tell you, oh mighty immortal being, that I've lost track of the amount of times I've been squeezed, grabbed, abused, and used for my body."

"I did not—" he wanted to respond, but I cut him off.

Again.

"Still not finished. What you see is a carefully designed image, created across years of trial and error. The first party I got invited to? Someone spiked my drink and I woke up abandoned in a bed with blood between my legs. So I learnt how to care for my drink and only have sealed water or beer. Boyfriends? Abusive motherfuckers. Most of them. Freaking millionaires pinching my ass and telling me the things they want to do to me while their wives are a few feet away? Thousands of them. And each time, I had to learn how to get over it and become the woman that I am today. And I built this shield piece by piece, over time and through horrible experiences. So that when I have important things to say, like save our fucking world because wales are cute, people will listen. And that's all I can do. Because I have nothing else. Once this finishes, I will lose it all, this *love* as they call it."

I scoffed at the ridicule of it all. "And what will remain of me? Nothing. I will be nothing. Because I have given so much, I cannot find myself underneath all the skins I had to wear. And if I ever managed to shed them all, I will find myself alone and forgotten, with no one to love me. And it will be okay, because deep down I know I am not deserving of that love."

My pulse sped up and I had to take a few deep breaths to

calm myself. What the hell did I just do? Did I just have a full on breakdown in front of a stranger? A faerie stranger, nonetheless? Fuck me.

"So if I want to eat a damn avo burger, I will do it without feeling any remorse or care about what you or anyone else might think," I added. "Just because." I took another bite of the food and let myself enjoy it, tasting every single piece my tongue touched while Rhy remained silent across from me. I wasn't even sure he was breathing.

Minutes passed and he let me finish my food without changing positions or speaking to me. From time to time I turned my attention to him and spotted his shocked gaze, still pointed at me. Did I just break the faerie?

"What, do you think *you* are worthy of love?" I finally spoke, while the server removed the empty plate from the table.

He swallowed hard before speaking. "I also had to build a shield across the years…"

So that was a hard no. I wasn't surprised, based on what I'd read about him and what Anwen told me. This guy enjoyed killing people. The embodiment of pain and suffering—or something, the internet called him.

"So why don't you just take the time to enjoy things? We're both doomed anyway, might as well live in the present and discover the wonders of the world we're living in," I raised my shoulders just slightly, as if I had the recipe of short-span-happiness. Which, in retrospect, I had. Trick your brain into thinking you are happy, enjoy small things every day, and it will help the illusion.

He remained silent for a short while, eyes still glancing at me, struggling to make a decision. After a while, he nodded.

"Alright sunshine, show me your world."

Day 3

I cannot explain how one thing led to another. Once we got past the hating each other phase, Rhylan and I started to connect. Enough to spend the entire afternoon chatting away and sharing ideas and controversial opinions, being brutally honest with what we disagreed on and after a stroll in the park, we went for dinner and now, here I was, wrapped in his arms. Dancing.

Neither of us wanted to opt for an early evening, so we prolonged the dinner as much as we could until, after the restaurant politely asked if we wanted our last drink, I suggested going to a club and as soon as Rhylan told me he hadn't been clubbing since the eighties; I knew there couldn't be a better option to end our evening with.

I took him to *Misto*, the club to go to, hosting VIP parties every night, where pretty much everyone who was someone liked to make an appearance. The fae left his jacket in the car, displaying an interesting neckline of tattoos, and surprisingly, I did not go home to change and remained in my boho golden dress, something very unusual for me. I did not trust him enough to take him home, nor did I want to risk bringing him back to the mansion where Anwen may still be working on her discoveries.

I did not know what she was up to, because my drunk self did not charge my phone last night and now it remained abandoned somewhere in the glove compartment. I wanted to give her as much time as I could, and enjoy myself in the process, because who the hell goes clubbing with a faerie? I had to test this man's limits.

Already used to skipping the queue, Rhylan headed to the main entrance while extending his arm to me to lead the way, and I giggled slightly. "Fancy life growing on you, Rhy?"

He turned and scanned me with a playful gaze. "Your light is that strong, sunshine. I can't stay away." I did not really get his meaning, but he just called me sunshine, which meant something good, so I let it be.

As soon as I got in, I spotted various celebs and other

influencers in the business, so I went and said hello, taking him with me and enjoying the reactions he stirred in everyone. Three actors looked at him with threatening stares, some kind of male turf war of the glances or something, while the women literally melted for him. As in, gripping his neck, touching his biceps and kissing his cheek. I could swear a Victoria Secret model even nibbled on his ear, all while I stood there and chatted with her partner. In response to that, Rhylan came closer to me and shifted away from the woman, stepping back and hugging me from behind. Almost as if he wanted to communicate that he was there with me. Or to show the woman that he belonged to someone and to leave him the heck alone.

Either way, there this huge man was, ravishingly beautiful and cuddled away from the mean girls who wanted a piece of that. I giggled and turned to snuggle into him, said goodbye, and led him to the dance floor. We remained surrounded by so many people, who were pushing us against each other so much that my chest became flattened against him and, noticing that no other conversation ensued, he seemed to finally relax. The tension in his shoulders slipped away and his palms started being playful again, making flicks around my hips.

We could not hear each other speak, only our gazes

communicating through the flashing lights, so after a song or two, during which Rhylan elegantly placed his weight from one foot to another in the rhythm of the music, making an attempt at dancing, he lowered his mouth to my ear.

"This is why I don't go clubbing anymore," he tried to explain, the rest of the words fading. I don't think he realised he needed to speak up for the sound of his voice to slash through the music and into my ear.

"I didn't take you for an old man. Is the old fae tired of the music of the youngsters?" I giggled back into his ear, using the appropriate amount of decibels to make sure my message was received. "Are you going to talk about the good old days?"

He threw me a shrewd gaze, then lowered his mouth to my ear once more, this time his breath tickling my skin. Sensation burst through me and were it not for the people pushing against us or the fact that his hands held me firmly attached to him, I would have probably lost my pace.

"I don't know how you do it. It's exhausting. And people are vulgar. I had my ass grabbed about ten times since we got here," he admitted, and I could not control my laughter. His face was tense for a second. Then, probably seeing my reaction, he allowed himself to smile as well.

"You wanted to see what the attention feels like," I

defended myself. "And I've been inappropriately touched about fifty times since we got here," I added, but instead of keeping the smile on his face, Rhy's jaw tensed and his brows furrowed. As a response, he cuddled me even closer, if such a thing was possible, wanting to keep me protected in a cocoon of his own making.

It was my turn to tense, because no one had ever thought that I needed to be cuddled and nestled away. Generally, every boyfriend or affair I had was very content to brag about me and let their friends dance or sit by my side, which always came with 'accidental' touches. I was used to it and knew how to control it and how to get away when someone became pushy. Truth be told, in the world of the famous, touching a woman's hips was more common than shaking her hand, so I wasn't all that bothered. I learnt my lessons and knew how to protect myself. Clearly, Rhylan didn't because his entire demeanour changed and my plan of relaxing and having fun was going to hell.

"Do you want to go to the sofas upstairs? It's not so crowded there," I made sure to add for grandpa, who probably had no clue about the upper section of the VIP stand.

As soon as he heard my words, his face illuminated and he nodded eagerly, then started pushing people away to make room for me. I took his hand and guided him up the stairs, passing the two bodyguards who had to slide a curtain for us to pass under.

Luckily, one of the sofas was empty, so we strolled to it and as soon as we sat, a bottle of champagne and two tall glasses appeared in front of us. Rhylan detensed, becoming curious yet again while I sipped from my glass, enjoying the coldness pouring down my throat.

"Why did we have to go through that, when we could have come here in the first place?" he frowned, then turned his attention to his own glass, picking it up and chugging it away with haste.

"Everyone is down there. People only come here to kiss and make up," I tilted my head towards another sofa, where a girl was straddling a middle-aged man.

Rhylan turned his gaze to what I was pointing, then grimaced. "Clubs…" he uttered with a long sigh.

"Hey, you are the one who wanted to taste *the life*," I repeated his own words back to him. "This is it."

Rhy shook his head slowly. "I am too old for this," he said, more to himself than to me. His features grew dark and he turned abruptly, uttering a determined apology.

"I am sorry about this afternoon." It took me a while to understand what he was saying.

"Don't, it's fine," I dismissed him quickly.

"I shouldn't have touched you without your permission," he continued, as if I hadn't even spoken, referencing how his hands slid on my hip when he first picked me up.

"Hey, I used my charm on you too. Tit for tat." I smiled and nudged him playfully with my shoulder.

"So, what do we do now?" Rhy asked.

As soon as he said the words, his eyes gleamed with the realisation, but my drunk self picked up the innuendo and oh baby, did my brain react to that. Before Rhylan could correct himself or add anything else, I turned to him and unashamedly placed my lips on his. Half of my face was numb so I wasn't very gentle. After a second or two, his own lips started moving against mine. Interweaving with my own and curiously tasting me. My tongue wanted to take control and moved inside his mouth, but at the contact, he jolted and stopped abruptly. His eyes were wide, so wide and he looked at me like he wanted nothing more in the world, like he craved for me with centuries of longing, yet his lips locked his mouth away .

"I'm sorry," he was the first to speak. He wanted to justify himself, despite that, I did not want to have it. And honestly, I was a bit too drunk to care.

"Rhylan, I need to ask something of you," I stopped him before hearing another explanation. Suddenly, the world started spinning. *How much did I drink?*

"Of course," he immediately said, to which I searched for my purse and picked out the keys. "You're driving again."

"Oh my god, where have you been, I was worried sick!" Anwen complained as I opened the door to her room. Rhylan had already left towards his, not before helping me up the stairs and kissing my hand again, making me feel like some sort of lost princess.

"Shhh," I said, my head throbbing. Why were the lights so bright? "We had a good time, that's all," I said and threw my heels across the room, toes enjoying the sensation of becoming alive again. Without taking off my dress or makeup, I threw myself in bed.

"He is amazing once you get to know him. He is chivalrous and nice, he knows everything about everything. Do you know he's met every single royal family in the world? Huh," I pulled my hair to the side and swished my neck around to make my bones crack and release some of the tension. "He is nice," I smiled into the pillow.

"Cressi, all this is supposed to be for his distraction, please do not get too excited about the guy," Anwen said carefully, though a feeling lingered at the back of her throat and I could not place it.

"You're right, he's not perfect. He doesn't like avocados." My friend looked at me with a frown and did not respond.

"Did you find anything?" I asked, struggling to keep my eyes open.

She started talking and explaining something about not being able to find... something. Her voice was soft and familiar, so I relaxed and drifted away to sleep.

Day 4

My hungover self, trying to have a filling breakfast in peace with Anwen and Rhy? Yeah... Not really happening. At first, Anwen was happy to have a late meal in the garden, as usual, but as soon as we took a seat and the baked goodies arrived, Rhylan made his appearance.

I welcomed him with a smile, yet Anwen looked like all the dark clouds had gathered over her head and instead of allowing her friend — the friend who sacrificed her entire day and night to babysit a faerie, not that I didn't enjoy it — to have a quiet recovery breakfast, she started snarling at Rhylan, who seemed to enjoy returning the favour.

I did not have a taste for this so early in the morning,

though the faerie was attentive enough to help me prepare my breakfast, cutting a few bits of fruit and settling them on my plate and then grabbing a piece of toast and a butter knife.

"Use the—"

"The vegan butter, I know," he smiled and nodded at me, eyes looking kinder than the day before. That sobered me up pretty quickly, and feeling a need to return the favour, I took his glass and served him orange juice.

We made the exchange and while passing me the slice of toast, his fingers lingered on mine a second longer than necessary. The freaking goose bumps started all over again, making my skin shiver at the contact. Yup, definitely too much alcohol, after all, we'd been drinking since early afternoon. And that's what all this was, just the familiarity we'd shared yesterday and the mojito bond that automatically forms between drinking buddies.

Anwen must have noticed our locked gazes, because she sighed in disgust. "Urgh, are you going to be like this every time, Rhy?" she pulled a mocking smirk at him and I quickly withdrew my fingers from his.

"Don't mock me, princess," he retorted. Instead of cracking a few more jokes at her expense, he pointed his gaze at the orange juice I'd offered. Like he didn't want to break the exchange we'd just made.

"Princess?" Anwen could not let it go. "What happened to sprout?" She raised her brows at him. I couldn't place if it was anger or curiosity that she transmitted. Either way, her eyes signalled hate.

I felt bad for him, because whatever his reasons, he cared for her in a way that I still needed to understand. He seemed annoyed at her most of the time, but also caring. Like if something happened right now, a lightning strike or an unpredictable thing, I knew he would lay himself in front of danger to protect Anwen. And like it or not, the guy was staying, so might as well let him enjoy it rather than attack him every chance she got. I understood her reasons though, based on what she'd told me, Rhy was nothing but the villain in her story.

"You don't like to be called a princess?" he caught her attack and retorted with double the speed.

"I do," I tried to dissipate some of the tension. Clearly, my opinion did not matter right now because they both seemed to ignore me. Alright fine, have it your way. I gave up listening and focused on the toast and orange juice in front of me.

After a few more back-and-forth attempts at hurting each other, which looked like an aggressive tennis match where the ball was made of insults, I stood from the chair and left them to their own, having had enough of their bickering for the rest of the day.

Only when I stepped away did they realise I was still there and stopped abruptly.

"Cressi," Anwen called after me. I waved and replied without looking back, "You two should be marketed as a pill to start headaches. I'm out."

Before either had a chance to protest, I left the garden and hurried back to the room to pick up my keys, then jumped in the car and drove back home. I hadn't stayed at the house in a long while and today, after all of this, I craved silence, so I headed out to my apartment, which was situated so high in the sky, I could spy on the buildings below.

"Morning Josh," I greeted the usher, who cracked some of his usual merry jokes and informed me of parcels he had placed inside the penthouse in the usual spot. I thanked him and went to the elevator, not at all concerned with whatever boxes waited for me. I needed today to be quiet. I did not feel like smiling for whatever product or trying out new things. My head was throbbing, but more importantly, the memory of the kiss I so easily dismissed the night before came creeping back.

The rejection. Of course he did not want me. After I'd told him the truth, I must have scared him away. Plus, he had some sort of weird vibe with my sister, and the last thing I wanted was to get between them.

I honestly wouldn't be surprised if I'd charged my phone and it would start to beep with details of the steamy hate sex they just had after I left. Not getting myself into that.

I unlocked the door and placed my purse on the small cabinet, threw the heels in the hallway and started walking barefoot on the marble floor, my soles happily stomping their way across.

After I got a bottle of water from the fridge and settled my phone onto the wireless charger in the bedroom, I headed to the living room, where I last remembered seeing my fuzzy slippers.

Only to be greeted by a huge gift basket, the most enormous thing I'd ever seen, carefully placed on the sofa table. I took a few steps towards it and realised it was filled with... plush whales? What the...

It took me a while to find the note in all that amalgam of plush marine life, but finally found a small envelope addressed to *Sunshine*.

My heart started thumping like crazy, because only one person called me that, and it happened to be just the day before.

I eagerly opened the envelope, to find a handwritten message, in an elegant writing. The likes of manuscripts displayed in museums from hundreds of years ago, with swirling, carefully placed letters.

I also think whales are cute.

Thank you for yesterday. It was the best time I had in a very long while. Coming from me, I'll let your wild imagination figure out the exact number.

Call me when you are in the mood for a surprise.
Rhy

A phone number followed on the back of the card.

He sent me a basket of whales, I giggled like a schoolgirl. Aware that I was smiling to myself like an idiot, I selected the biggest one from the basket and gave it a tight hug, the softness of the plush warming my chest, then headed to the bedroom and buried myself under the blankets, holding the whale tightly. For whatever reason, I felt a little less lonely.

Day 5

"Ready for that surprise you promised."

It took me two hours of rushing around the apartment, changing three outfits and dropping my phone a few times until I finally decided to send the text. I typed it over and over, struggling to find the words that made me sound excited yet not desperate, intrigued but not falling off my feet. When I hit the send button, my heart drummed viciously almost to the point of thinking I was having a heart attack. Fortunately, less than a minute later the buzzing made me jump and hurry to the vanity where I threw my phone on.

"I was hoping to have a good day today, glad to know it will be full of sunshine. Good morning."

He texted back. In less than a minute. Using a happy face.

I wondered who still used a smiling face nowadays, yet I quickly came to appreciate a centuries old faerie sliding through all the yellow faces to find the most appropriate one.

Sunshine emoji sent along with "Good morning Rhy"

"Sleep well?" he pinged me back seconds later.

"One of the whales you sent kept me company. You?"

"Terrible. I heard Anwen snoring through the walls all night long." Wink emoji. I could not contain my laughter.

"I bet she would love to hear that." Another wink emoji.

"What time should I pick you up?"

So eager Rhy, I smiled to myself. "An hour is good."

"Address?"

I texted him the address of a cafe two blocks away. I never gave my address, not until I trusted the person and even then, I preferred my guests to notify reception of their arrival. Safety first.

My phone started buzzing. This time it was Anwen. Via video. I smiled, noticing how quickly news must travel in that house. It made me remember the days when Erik lived two rooms away. How he spied on us to the extent that he would message me ten minutes after we thought we had successfully snuck out of the house to tell me he would come pick us up by five in the morning. He always helped disguise our drunken arrival.

Now, Anwen seemed to be the one spying on Rhy.

"Morning, sexy," I replied.

"Hey bestie, what are you up to?"

"Nothing much, just getting ready." I replied and waited for her questions. Which did not seem to come.

"Wanna go for lunch or something?" Anwen offered, probably feeling the need to compensate for yesterday's disastrous breakfast.

"Can't, I have to be somewhere in an hour."

"Ugh, okay, maybe we can go out in the afternoon," she suggested and I nodded. Then I noticed her smiling face changing into a grimace. "The bastard is at the door. Call you back."

"Bye" I only had time to say.

Another minute later, a text from Rhylan popped up on my screen. I giggled, these two were going to drive me mad. "What car do I want?"

"I don't know. What car do you want?" I replied back.

"Anwen is asking and I don't know what to say."

"Do you go by colour or by model?" I sent back.

"Sunshine, you are already aware of my affinity for black."

"Black...okay. If you wanna feel like batman, go for the Valkyrie. It's Jason's new toy."

"Let me know, cause I'll have to change my outfit for that car." I sent back straight away. No high heels in the martins, I hated how I had to fold my legs and my ankles ended up hurting long before I reached the destination.

"She's giving me the Chiron. Is that good?"

"Yup, I can work with that." I sent him a smiling face and a race emoji.

"Be there in twenty minutes." He texted back.

Seeing Rhylan leaning against the car did a weird thing to my stomach. He chose black pants with a black shirt, unbuttoned at the neck, that cupped his biceps perfectly and wore a watch that looked as expensive as the car. Perfectly polished shoes. If I were to take a picture of him right now, I would definitely break the internet. Kardashians my ass.

I saw how his eyes illuminated at the sight of me and had to stop the urge to run into his arms and kiss him again. The fear of rejection stopped me in my tracks.

As soon as I approached, he leaned forward and, because of his height, he had to bend more than a little to reach my cheek and place a soft kiss on my skin. *Don't blush, don't blush, don't blush.* I hoped I had enough foundation to cover any signs of unwanted colour popping into my cheeks and quickly made my way inside the car, through the door he held open for me.

"Where did you learn to drive?" My mouth released the words before I had time to think them properly. Nonetheless, it was a good question.

"On route sixty-six," he answered as he backed away and waited for the cars to pass so he could pull into traffic. "In the forties," he added with a proud smirk, like the information would do something to me. And oh my goodness, it did. Seeing this man rest his wrist on the steering wheel may be the sexiest gesture I witnessed. Ever.

"What's the surprise?" I quickly asked, pushing away dirty thoughts from my mind.

"It's a place I picked specially for you," he glanced at me and threw me an excited smile. And I struggled to breathe. *The fuck am I getting myself into?*

We spent the next twenty minutes in silence, however not the awkward kind. It felt comfortable being around him and even though the only communication we had during this time were exchanged glances and smiles; it felt like we were saying it all. I enjoyed being in his company and by the glances he was sending in my direction, while perfectly navigating without a GPS as though he had leisurely spent time in the city, he was also relaxed with me.

A strain lingered on his shoulders every time Anwen was nearby, something so unnoticeable that I doubted even he realised. It felt nice to see that tension vanishing when it was just the two of us.

Pulling me from my thoughts, Rhylan drove the car into an underground parking lot and since I was so preoccupied with admiring the faerie, I had absolutely no idea where we were. Nor did I want to make my lack of attention obvious by asking him.

"Ready for your surprise?" he displayed a full smile, then quickly exited the car and hurried to open the door for me. I didn't know what it was with him and opening doors. Very few men had paid attention to me up to such minor details, so I might as well enjoy it and reap the fruits of his old age.

"How old are you, Rhy?" I bombarded him with the question as soon as he displayed himself on my side of the car, reaching a hand to help me get out without placing a wrong step.

His eyes widened for a second, two, three. Then he remained frozen. The question had shaken him somehow.

"No one asked me that." He blinked a few times. "Ever."

"Well, I am asking now," I smiled and grabbed his hand to help pull me out of the car, then realised my scrambled mind and bent down again to find my purse. All the while, he remained paralysed by my side.

"So?" I pushed as I slammed the car door closed and it

announced locking with a beep. "I mean, I assume you will need a lot of candles on your cake," I giggled and pushed him slightly with my elbow, taking the lead towards the elevator.

He followed in silence, one that he kept even as another set of doors opened for us.

"Are you seriously not gonna tell me? Do you think I will freak out or something?"

Rhylan turned to me then, his body towering over mine, eyes scanning me like he was seeing me for the first time. Then he blinked and part of the darkness faded away, making his features more relaxed, honest.

"I don't know," he said.

"I won't. I promise I will not freak out," I assured him. The internet said he was centuries old, so worst case, he had sex with Cleopatra or something. That would be a good story.

"I honestly don't know…"

"Oh come on Rhy, I will not freak out! Trust me," I pushed again.

He chuckled, his laughter leading the way to fluttering in my stomach, then spoke again. "Sunshine, I do not know how old I am," he admitted with a small grimace.

"Oh." I stopped for a beat. How could he not know? It was so easy to pinpoint any era of time nowadays; we only had to ask Google.

"What's the last thing you remember?" I quizzed him.

"Darkness, cold, loneliness. I lived on my own for a while, with a band of warriors after my father was murdered. They trained me every day to the brink of death until I was ready to enter the kingdom. I don't know how long the training was, could be years or centuries."

"And your mom?"

"Returned to the god at childbirth," he answered with an even tone like he was reading a statistic report.

"And when you got out in the world, what was happening?" I hoped to form some kind of timeline.

"Water and Wind had become allies," he responded.

"No, with humans. What were they doing? Any important events in history?"

He frowned, trying to think back and after a long while, he finally said. "The Roman Empire still existed. There was a pope, John of some number who was taken down by the ruler." I saw him scrambling his mind for more details and coming up with nothing else.

"OK, give me a sec..." I started typing frantically. When in doubt, Google is your bestie. Link after link, site after site, I went through the Roman Empire and popes until I found what I was looking for. Or the closest thing to it, at least.

"962 AD," I started reading out loud, *Otto the Great was*

crowned Holy Roman Emperor by Pope John XII. Otto ended the anarchy in Rome by soon appointing his own Pope. He revived the power of the Western Roman Empire. So we can assume you were an adult by then, and give or take a few years or centuries... I turned to him and smiled, proud of myself. "We're both millennials."

Rhylan deepened his frown, but somehow it made him look cute rather than menacing. "You know, millennials? I'm a millennial, you are a millennial? Kinda..." I asked, hopeful.

"Sunshine, I have no idea," he chuckled.

I sighed. "Millennials are a generation of people who live to see the turn of a new millennium. So as you were alive in the tenth century and you are alive now, you've seen two millennia go by. So you're a millennial. Make sense?"

He looked at me in surprise and blinked so many times that I thought I might have damaged a circuit in his brain until he tilted his head back and started laughing with a joy I'd never heard anyone reach before. I could not help myself and did the same.

"A millennial," he said after his laughing fit calmed down a bit. "I'll take it," he approved with a grateful smile.

"Now that we established your generation, does your surprise consist of being locked in an elevator?"

Rhylan looked at me stupefied, then smirked and reached

to press the elevator button, which immediately started rumbling and pulling us up.

"Oh my god, are you telling me we just sat in an elevator for the past ten minutes?" I sighed, covering my face with my hands in the ultimate sign of how-stupid-can-I-be. Rhylan stepped closer to me and wrapped an arm around my waist to catch my attention back.

"Don't worry about it, it's what millennials do," he replied with a grin.

We both started laughing again.

When the elevator reached up, the doors opened to reveal the surprise. It was my turn to look dumbfounded

"The museum of broken things?" I read the sign aloud and looked at him inquisitively.

He raised his shoulders. "I thought it would be a nice addition to yesterday's conversation," he said and I cringed internally at the memory of how I'd basically told him we were both broken and undeserving of love during a mini breakdown at the lunch table.

"I was hoping you forgot that…" I sighed.

"Come on, it will be fun," he nudged me again with his shoulder. "Two broken beings, admiring broken things…" He waved with a sudden whiff of excitement, but I frowned and looked at him in disbelief. The nerve on this man.

His next words were my undoing. "It's what millennials do."

That was it. I could not contain my laughter, so we sat there, on the entry hallway, laughing out loud for minutes. Unashamedly, like I hadn't done in a long time, and when we finally calmed down, Rhy escorted me inside and bought the tickets.

For the next two hours, I clung to his arm and watched different displays, feeling just a little less broken.

"I'll text you the address and leave a ticket for you at the entrance," I said as I got out of the car after having spent the afternoon with Rhy. Following the museum visit, we added a late lunch that once again had turned into dinner and I ended up inviting him to a fashion show I was attending the next day. As a lingerie model. I conveniently left that part out.

"Or, if you prefer, my sister can bring you, though I'm not sure how a car journey with you and Anwen will go down. You'll be bickering and driving into a pole."

The playful smile on his face faltered to the extent that his entire face turned white, all colour vanishing from sight. I didn't have time to enquire more because my phone started ringing, the caller ID announcing a brand I had just signed a contract with.

"Sorry, I gotta take this. Jason and Elsa will be there too, they can bring you," I said to him instead of a goodbye.

Day 6

"I would kill for your boobs, girl," Anwen exclaimed as a form of greeting when she entered my changing room and found me in a very tight bra, fitted with way too many push-up pads that basically brought the ladies up to my neck. They were a nice pair, I would not deny that and I liked what the mirror showed.

My abs needed a little work, though with the hip tattoo running down my right thigh and the silver brazilians they shoved me in, I looked good. Real good. I only needed to tie the cape which I then had to theatrically release onto the stage and display myself on the catwalk, stop at the centre stage in three photo poses, another two at the end of the catwalk, turn, walk, slide my hair to the right, then stop at the base, last pose, exit stage towards the left making room for the next model. Piece of cake.

"I would kill for your plump ass, but you didn't wanna show it tonight," I retorted and rose from my seat in front of the mirror to greet her with a quick hug, careful not to tangle our hairdo.

Anwen looked amazing as well. She had come to receive a check for her foundation and had specifically chosen a dark green opera dress and adorned it with a set of emerald earrings and a tear diamond necklace. Elegance at its finest.

"Elsa must be brimming at the sight of you," I smiled, thinking about how proud her mother would be at finally seeing her look like a princess.

"Actually, dad was the one to make a big show of it. He thinks I just made two mill," my friend giggled.

"How are things with Rhylan?" I hadn't checked my phone, so I didn't know if he texted or called and I felt bad about the way I abandoned him yesterday. I was scheduled to do a live on Insta with the brand that called, which ended at two in the morning, so I had to reject all three of his calls and I very much doubted he had gone to Anwen to check on me or that he even knew about the existence of the gram.

"Ugh... the bastard was so quiet today and in a bad mood.

I don't know if he slept wrong or what. He kept to himself during the drive here and at breakfast he was plainly mean. Brooding about something. I honestly don't care, I'm only counting the days to get him out of here and get my boyfriend back," she sighed, although, for the first time in the longest, her eyes gleamed with hope. Even a dash of excitement.

I smiled at her encouragingly and caressed her shoulder. "You'll see him soon."

"I can't wait," she giggled, making tiny jumps from the excitement.

"If he were to see you right now... my, my..." I added with a suggestive wiggle of my brows.

"Honestly, I'm scared he would be blinded by you!" she replied amused, "You look fantastic!"

I smiled and thanked her.

"Did you invite anyone today? That theatre guy?"

"No, I didn't feel like it, haven't spoken to him since I got back from LA. He was just good packaging," I raised my shoulders in defeat.

"As soon as I get Ansgar back, I'll ask him to bring you to the Earth Kingdom and we can go hunting for sexy faerie men. You need to try one, I swear!" Her eyes went wide with excitement and I chuckled again. My sister had turned into me. I was usually the one to treat men the way they treated us, but here Anwen was, selling the heck out of sex with a faerie.

Rhylan's lips were on my neck and his hand trailed teasingly on my hip, fingers dragging lower towards in between my thighs while his tongue teased my skin and the shell of my ear.

"Look at what you do to me, sunshine," he confessed while pinning me against the vanity, my pelvis pushing back from the pressure. Pushing back into him. Into his hardness, which I felt through the fabric of his trousers. Throbbing for me, so close that I could feel it down my—

"Well, are you?"

"Huh?"

Anwen looked at me with surprise. "Inviting him here? The theatre guy?"

"What?" It took me a moment to return to reality. "No, no, I'm not. Sorry, Anwen, I need to find the designer to help me place this cape. See you after?"

Before she had a chance to reply, I grabbed the ornate robe and ran out the door before my friend realised what had just happened. Before I, myself, did.

I couldn't be doing this. I couldn't think about Rhy like this, not in broad daylight and especially not in front of the girl he clearly had some sort of feelings for. I needed to control this, needed to get better at it and stay away from that faerie. A man who had made me laugh like no one did, gave me his undivided attention and looked at me as though I was the most interesting person in the world.

Of course he's good at flirting. He had a thousand years to practice it; I convinced myself. Calm your tits!

Never better said because five minutes later I was making my way onto the catwalk, feeling and looking like a queen. Those moments were the peak of my year. I felt invincible. There I was, higher than anyone else, basically on a very long pedestal and all the eyes were on me. The bad part was that there were so many lights I could barely see the stage and where I was supposed to direct my next step, let alone the expressions of the people around. Either way, I liked to imagine their gobsmacked faces at my beauty and confidence.

Hashtag girl power

"You look radiant, sunshine," Rhylan came up from behind me while I was unpinning my hair in the vanity.

"Oh god, please not again," I sighed to myself.

I closed my eyes and pressed my fingers together in a self-motivating stance. I paused, wishing Rhylan away, then opened my eyes again. To see him still there, gazing at my reflection in the mirror with a curious look.

"Rhylan?" I retorted the inquisitive gaze, which made him raise his brows.

"Yes?" he responded with no small amount of surprise.

"What are you doing here?" The rest was implied. In my cabin, with me half-naked. My mind raced to the remaining part of my fantasy and wondered if he truly was hard for me.

Rhylan pulled my hair to one side and away from my shoulder, then gently, so slowly, pressed his lips on my skin and I exploded with the sensation, releasing a very steamy breath that must have sounded like a low moan. It made Rhy's eyes turn a dark obsidian, something savage overpowering them and turned me abruptly to him, pressing me against his chest, against his very hot body and against... damn, he really was hard for me.

"You look like a goddess, sunshine," he murmured and released a low breath himself, hands shaking slightly on my hips and fingers moving millimetrically. It gave the impression that they wanted to push further, to explore me, yet he struggled to control his impulses.

Well, he might have to do it, but not me. If he wanted to play, then I was most willing. Without saying a word, I raised on my tiptoes, because even on extra-high heels I could not reach him properly and placed my lips on his.

As soon as we connected, butterflies released from my stomach and my hands jumped to him, across his shoulders, fingers interlocked in his hair, while my mouth pushed savagely onto him, tongue finding his taste. He reminded me of mint and some sort of spice, the most uniquely tasting kiss I have ever enjoyed.

For a while, he just stood there, only moving his tongue and lips, the rest of his body too surprised by my confidence, by the way I was claiming his kisses. After his tongue did a particular twist I had never encountered before and I released a moan into his mouth, he became possessed.

Rhy's hands trailed along my ass, squeezing with eagerness, moving around and exploring parts of my body he hadn't had access to before, then trailed along my back and one of them returned to my ass, grabbing it underneath my panties while the other went towards my breasts. He extended his palm so widely that he was able to touch parts of them both, too eager to feel them for the first time to bother with giving them individual attention. Then his hand trailed down again and, oh yes baby, please do. I spread my legs to give him better access, though the movement broke the trance and abruptly, Rhy unhooked himself from me and took a step back. He was a sight. His lips red, eyes pinned on me and that hardness poking through his pants in such a way that my stomach dropped, knowing instantly that what Anwen said about faeries must be true.

In between rapid pants, Rhylan took another step back. And another. "We can't—" He stopped to breathe again and took a step forward, towards me, battling his previous decision, then reconsidered and extended the distance in between us once more. His eyes were wild with desire and he kept shaking his head, convincing himself of whatever choice he had just made.

"Anwen—" he said in a hush tone. It was all I needed to hear. I never guessed that a single word, a name that I loved, would have the power to break me in such a way.

"Get out," I murmured.

"I need to tell you…" he tried to explain but I did not want to hear it.

"You listen here, bastard, this is not an all you can eat buffet, this is a motherfucking five star restaurant with a month long waiting list. For both Anwen and I. You can't just come in here and mess both of us around," I screamed at him. I usually avoided conflict and I abhorred people who retorted to raising their voice in a fight, yet this had me.

"Sunshine, let me explain. I really want this, more than I

wanted anything in— I don't even remember," he tried to explain.

"Of course you do, motherfucker. I was there for her! I was there when my sister came back home more broken than when she left, I was there to witness her tears and all the pain you caused! So don't think that you can come in here and do it all over again, because I won't let you. I will kill you myself before you hurt her again."

He stopped and... smiled. With pride. "You are everything I hoped you would be," his breath became even again, like he had found some kind of inner peace.

"Get out!" I shouted but he did not react.

"Get out!" I ordered, but seeing how he was determined to continue to invade my privacy, I turned to the vanity and snatched the first heavy thing I spotted. My makeup bag.

And threw it right in his face.

Of course I didn't sleep in my own bed and I didn't do it alone. For the first time in as long as I could remember, I wasn't able to go to Anwen's when I had my heart broken, because the reason I felt like that, lived right next to her. And I would not bring any more issues to that poor girl, who had already so much to deal with and who warned me, multiple times, not to get attached to Rhylan because he is a conniving bastard.

Here I was, fantasizing about the villain of the story and getting hurt in the process. Once he left my changing room, I spent a long time in the shower, washing away every part of me that he touched, but even an hour later, I still felt his hands draping over my hips. And what's the best cure for heartache?

A fashion show after party.

I drowned myself in alcohol for hours and picked the best looking man at the party to make me forget about my sorrows. I will not deny it, the fact that he was packed with muscles and had short dark hair made it even better.

I snuck out the following day at about five in the morning and headed to the radio station where I was supposed to take part in an interview, all the while feeling like the dirtiest woman to walk the face of this earth and thankful for the huge amount of perfume and wet wipes I stashed in my car for emergency situations. Three hours later, still wearing the make-up and hairdo from the fashion show — or what was left of it after the rough sex session — I finally reached my building, where tiny angels playing harps welcomed me back home. I vividly dreamt about a warm bath to soak into for hours and forget about everyone and everything.

Of course, my plans did not come as expected, because as soon as I got out of the car, Rhylan appeared in front of me. Wearing jeans. And a black shirt.

It was odd seeing him switch to a modern outfit, but my heart started fluttering at the sight of him. Both because he was sexy as fuck, and also because I was still angry with him.

"Nope, I'm not doing this," I said instead of a greeting and walked past him and up the stairs, where the usher had already opened the door for me.

"Cressida, we need to talk," he insisted and although I didn't see him, I knew he was chasing after me, so I hurried through the door and made my way inside, hoping he could not pass security.

Yet Alex let him through. The new boy was not cut out for the job, too kind to everyone and everything. I didn't doubt he even welcomed Rhylan with a smile. Also, the new usher was probably a foot shorter than Rhylan, so I guessed that helped, too.

"Stop it! Stop it right there!" I halted abruptly and turned back to Rhylan, a finger raised in the air.

"Is there a problem, Miss Thompson?" Nigel must have heard me making a scene and he blissfully hurried from his desk to come check it out. I didn't know if the main security guy had a gun. I'd seen the taser on his belt, so at least I had that to feel a little safer.

"Sunshine... please," Rhylan's eyes chased my own and I spotted surprise and a dash of hurt in them. I did not care. I was not having any of this.

"Rhylan, do not be a creep. We're done. I do not want to speak to you again and I am asking you to leave right now." I tried to get some reason into him, because as soon as Nigel approached us, Rhy's eyes went wild. Sheer anguish made its way to his features and I honestly could not anticipate his next move.

"Cressida," he addressed me, though his eyes remained pinned on the security guard, his right hand making a fist, and I immediately started fearing for the employee's safety. Because this was a thousand year old faerie whom the internet said cannot die.

"Rhylan," I spoke again, starting to get a bit panicked with what I'd caused. I hated conflict and the last thing I wanted was to put either Nigel, Alex, or myself in danger. "If you do not leave immediately, Nigel here will call the police. Seeing how you are trespassing a private property, you will be arrested. The only reason I do not want you in jail is Anwen and what that might cause to the agreement you two have." I kept my voice levelled and spoke clearly and with decision, like I was doing a commercial, putting my best tone forward. "So please leave, and stop making a fool of yourself," I pushed, hoping to get some sense into him.

His obsidian eyes carried the weight of the world when he gazed at me once more, our eyes locking for a few seconds, my serene blue ones meeting the darkness exuding from his own. He lowered them and with a simple nod, turned back and left the building.

I exhaled, but did not find any relief in doing so. His

disappointed gaze pierced through me, making my stomach sink with dread and for whatever reason, I blamed myself for how the situation was handled. I should have stayed outside and talked to him, I should have explained my reasons and acted like an adult, rather than a hurt teenager. He had chosen my sister over me.

Of course he did. They had history, had known each other for a year and he left everything behind to follow her and spend more time with her. His choice made the most sense and if I were to be honest, between Anwen and myself, I would have chosen her a thousand times over as well. That gave me no right to treat him the way I did, especially since he had come to talk about it, yet here I was, acting like a silly teen, rejected for the first time. Second, if we are to count the kiss from the club that first night.

"Miss Thompson?" Nigel called my name.

"Huh?" I turned and saw that he looked at me with concern. "Yeah, I'm okay, thank you Nigel. I'll just go home now."

"Do you need us to call someone or escort you upstairs?" The man tried to offer, so I shook my head abruptly. I wanted none of that. Only to be alone.

"No thank you, I'll be alright."

Before he had a chance to add anything else, I hurried

inside the open doors of the elevator and pressed my key card to the penthouse button.

As soon as I unlocked the door, my usual routine started. I threw my bag on the entry table, shoes in the hallway and because I was feeling particularly disgusting today, I shimmied out of my dress and unclasped my bra, letting the girls spring free. Panties went off as well.

Ugh, I needed to get that guy's sweat off my skin. And needed to burn those clothes.

"Such a marvellous view you have here, sunshine," I heard a voice and, oh my god, Rhylan was in my living room. Sitting on my favourite armchair, holding a drink, comfortably resting an ankle over his knee and looking directly at the entrance door. Thus, on my naked self.

"What the fuck!" I exclaimed and covered my boobs with one hand while extending my other palm as wide as I could to cover in between my legs. I quickly crouched to the floor and shimmied back into the dress I had worn for about twenty hours now.

Only then I turned to him. "What are you doing here?" I accused.

"Waiting for you, of course," he responded with a sly smile, then took another sip of his drink. *His drink.*

No, no, no, no, no, no. No. I spotted the bottle on the table, dad's Remy Martin collector's bottle. I thought I must be imagining things.

He didn't.

He wouldn't.

An image of dad's proud smile when he brought the brandy home came to mind. How he'd placed it on the display shelf, his chest brimming with self-esteem, a feeling I was too young to understand. How mom hurried into his arms and kissed him for the award he'd received, which accompanied the bottle. It symbolised their love, those moments I thought I had all my life to witness, that were stolen from me so suddenly.

I hurried to the table and fell on my knees in front of it, picking up the opened bottle, my hands shaking so hard I could barely hold it. Some of the liquid was missing.

"Rhylan, what are you drinking?" I barely escaped the words, but I knew. There was no need for him to answer because I knew. I turned to him abruptly with tears in my eyes and saw the exact moment when his smug face turned to concern.

"That was my father's bottle, you sick fuck!" I screamed at him, tears now rushing down my face.

Oh my god, he opened dad's bottle. Oh, my god.

"Cressida?" I heard him shifting in the seat and the sound

of crystal stomping on the floor.

"Cressida!" I felt him rush to me and catch me as my body suddenly turned into lead and I lost control over my own muscles. My vision turned dark and my head tilted back. I felt it and couldn't do anything about it.

"Cressida!" His voice called me back, redirecting the entirety of my attention towards him and the terrified expression on his face. "Cressida, breathe!" He commanded and I did just that. Once, twice, three times, taking deeper and deeper breaths until the world around me stabilised, the tears in my eyes fading away.

What a strange occurrence, I hadn't cried in years, yet the image of one of my father's most prized possessions was the trigger I needed. It took a minute or two for my eyes to become less glazy and for me to fully recover. Damn, I'd almost fainted, or at least, I think that's what it was.

"Are you alright?" Rhylan's hand cupped my chin while the other sustained my weight from behind, pressing at my back.

I nodded and tried to stand, his body offering the support I needed to push my muscles upwards. "It's a collector's bottle, there are only about fifty in the world now and that was my father's," I explained. It probably made no sense to him to go this crazy over a nice bottle of brandy.

"It was my father's," I said again, like that would miraculously sort out everything.

Rhylan helped me take a seat on the sofa and carefully laid himself next to me, all the while giving me enough distance to calm down and take air into my lungs.

"Cressida, I am so sorry," he said, still panicked by my reaction, "I wanted to make a big theatrical impression on you and didn't even think. Idiot," he scolded himself and for some reason, it made me chuckle.

"How the hell did you get in here?" I looked at him in disbelief, my initial reaction coming back to me.

"I used my powers," he stumbled over the words, showing nothing of the big impression he had planned. "I can vanish from one place to another. It's complicated, but I had to break in the first time so I can connect to this place. Which... sorry about that," he pursed his lips with an apology.

"And why are you here?"

"We need to talk. I need to explain to you what happened. My plan was to appear here, possibly tie you to the bed and make you listen," he admitted and somehow, I knew he wasn't lying. Tie me to the bed? Things would have gotten interesting, to say the least.

"And now?" I asked with curiosity. "Now that you messed up your big entrance, what do you plan on doing?"

"I would still like to talk, if that's alright with you. I also must confess I didn't expect to smell another man's lingering desire on you, which, I will not lie, is very distracting."

My face dropped and I had to swallow a dry lump from my throat.

"Fuck…" I said again.

"I am not the jealous type, still, it makes me want to find the man and rip his dick off to make sure it never touches you again, and then come back and show you what real pleasure feels like," he smirked, though his eyes shone darker than usual.

OK, from all the shades of crimson, how do I order the darkest one? This faerie could smell the guy and knew I had sex. Creepy. So, so creepy.

"He was Henry Cavill's stunt double. Can you honestly blame me?" My self-defence system blurted out, and okay, I'll take it, it was a nice save.

"Clearly, I was planning on showering, which is why I removed all my clothes at the door, yet someone felt the need to be stalkery and drink dad's brandy," I accused and his face faltered again. "Also Rhylan, why are you here? Why is it so important that we talk?"

"Because sunshine, the last woman I loved, over a century ago, was a queen. But when I met you, I understood I found myself a goddess."

"You really thought Anwen was my sister?" After feeling recovered enough to walk, though Rhylan insisted on escorting me to the bedroom and even waited by the bathroom door, shouting through it from time to time to make sure I was still ok, I changed into some comfy leggings and a t-shirt. After I came out, Rhylan took a seat on the floor, giving me the bed and looking up at me while I brushed my hair.

He appeared less tense and I didn't know if it was because he had adopted modern clothes or simply because he sat there and looked at me as if I was something precious, but it made him young and unworried.

Like he was finally taking the time to release whatever held him back and the fact that he had someone to be honest with, to remove the mask he always wore, made his eyes sparkle with joy. I loved seeing him like that.

He nodded as I echoed the explanation he gave me for yesterday's rejection. Because I referred to my bestie as my sister so many times, he thought we were blood related and stopped from fear of 'messing things up.'

I blinked a couple of times and sighed deeply. "You know, you are the first man to see me without makeup in... seven years, maybe? Apart from Erik."

"Did you two…" he didn't say the words, didn't have to because I understood the question and this time, I was the one to enjoy talking to a complete stranger about something I always had to keep to myself.

"We weren't together, officially, but it was always something there. Whenever both of us were single, we acted on it. I think we both enjoyed having that person there to love unconditionally, because we'd known each other for such a long time and didn't really consider the possibility of one of us not being there. In my mind, I always thought I'd end up with Erik. He was my first love, my first everything." I confessed, releasing some of the grains that caused heaviness in my chest. Memories I never had anyone to share with.

"I bet Anwen took it well," he huffed.

"Rhy, it's a secret you will carry to your grave," I abruptly turned my expression ferociously serious and gazed at him with threat.

"Noted."

A pause. We finished the pleasantries, the going around the subject while keeping on it, because even though Rhylan thought I was Anwen's sister, it still didn't explain his reaction.

"Are you ready?" he settled more comfortably on the floor, even though I insisted at least three times for him to take a chair. Rhylan shook his head very determined and aligned the soles of his feet in a perfect resting yoga pose. That must be some very flexible denim.

I copied his pose as much as I could and inhaled a long breath in, preparing myself for whatever was about to come, then nodded.

"Believe it or not, it starts in the Evigt Forest. I was assigned there over a hundred and fifty years ago to find a powerful source of energy of the earthling kingdom, which is believed to be hidden in their goddess' burial place. I'm sure you know about the particularities of the place since Anwen lived there for a while, so I will not bore you with details. It was easier to enter back then. There were no restrictions or guards. I honestly didn't expect to find any people inside.

But there it was, this cabin full of soldiers and maids. I was more curious back then, so I had to find out who lived in the woods and why they were so guarded. I met Louise one night, when she escaped her guards and went for a walk under the moonlight."

"So you truly loved a queen?" I asked, remembering what

he had said. I especially liked the part about me being a goddess. Be that as it may, I wasn't going to steal his thunder.

"She was wild and adventurous back then and missed her country and her family greatly. She was the only other human, apart from you, who knew who I was and treated me like a regular being, accepting my flaws and ideas. We had an affair for many years, blissful years of my existence. The times she had to return to the castle were grim, so I occupied myself with investigation and when she returned, I lived for her company. She brought me a uniform and I posed as her personal guard, accompanying her in strolls around the forest. It was the easiest way for us to spend time together and keep her from unsuspecting eyes," he explained.

"And how was that? Dating a queen?" I carefully added.

Rhylan's lips brought a sweet smile to his face and I understood that even now, he still held affection for the royal. He must have loved her deeply.

"While it lasted, it was perfect. She had a very inquisitive mind, just like you, and—" he paused and gazed at me, "just like you, she asked millions of questions about the past and humanity, culture and religion. Her questions were based more on politics than historical figures, even so, you two are alike in that way," he turned to me and smiled.

I reciprocated and giggled even louder at the memory of

his reactions at all the questions I'd bombarded him with while we were visiting the museum. "What was the Venice Carnival like? Was Casanova really that good in bed? How did Marie Antoinette keep her hair up like that? When did you see a poodle for the first time and so, so many others. He had laughed and shared the information gleefully, sometimes telling me the answers I wanted and others, admitting he had absolutely no idea.

"We had been intimate so many times that it became natural. We knew our wants, knew each other's bodies almost as well as our own. All it took was a slip on my behalf. It ended in pregnancy. I protested, worrying for her safety, but Louise knew how much I wanted heirs, how long I had craved for the idea of sharing my blood, that she decided to take the risk."

I was looking at him with so much interest that I ended up breathing at the same time he did, coordinating our every move from fear to miss any minor detail. This was a part of history that only I had access to and I would not miss a beat. Reading the question from my expression, Rhy continued.

"The king obviously found out and was not willing to accept the child as his own, and forbade her return to the forest. The day she left for the palace was the last time I saw her. I could not be her personal guard when entire battalions had no idea who I was. The servants must have guessed by then, anyway. That is when the king commanded the forest to be protected.

The locals thought it was a piece of heaven since being with me for so long had preserved Louise's youth and destroyed the territory as much as they could. They actually did me a favour because the earthlings were devastated for a good decade or two back then. Either way, the protection of the forest was a lie. The king hated the betrayal so much, he wanted to forbid anyone to step inside, so he closed the territory and made a proclamation asking future rulers to do so as well. Those damned faeries have enjoyed the peace and quiet since then," he grumbled.

"What happened to the baby?" I asked below my breath.

"This is the part you need to brace yourself for," he announced.

"Okay…"

"The child, being a bastard, was removed from the palace. A boy, I found out years later, after Louise passed away. He grew up on a farm in the North. When the king's son found out about the existence of a brother, he visited the location and gifted him a fortune, dispatching him to America to help him start a new life. I had to blindly chase after that with little luck. You see, our genes differ from humans, to the point that the genetic heritage skips seven generations. So someone born of me would inherit my powers seven generations later. Only then, once they are of age and strong enough, I can sense the connection and find them," he stopped and scanned me, raising his brows half-way through, like he was waiting for me to put the puzzle together. And so I did.

"So seven generations, from say 1850... means that the person is alive today," I answered for him.

"It means that my true heir, the one that has my bloodline and also inherited my power, my true born heir, is alive today," he confirmed.

Okay, wow, that was a lot of information to take in. So Rhylan was in NYC looking for his heir, which made sense. But he was spending all this time with me and Anwen, and her family.

"Oh my god," my eyes went wide while his own lost their tension abruptly. Of course, it made so much sense. The Odstars came from Sweden, with a grand-grand-grandfather that started this gigantic business that turned into an empire for generations to come, and Jason was constantly bragging about his origins and connection with the royal family. They even sent each other Christmas cards for crying out loud. "Oh my god," I repeated again to myself.

"I'm sure Anwen told you about my encounter with Erik,"

Rhy finally spoke again, probably after my features settled enough for him to do so. "I didn't expect to find him so quickly, yet as soon as he turned twenty-seven, which is the equivalent of fae maturity, I sensed him. And I connected to him."

"Wh… wh… what? Aren't we talking about Jason here?" I almost shouted with surprise.

"Jason is sixth generation," he replied calmly, and his answer almost made me faint again.

"Anwen is your daughter???"

Whatever words came out of my mouth did the opposite of the previous sentence and instead of shouting, I wasn't even sure I spoke them.

He nodded elegantly. "You now understand my hesitance. The kiss at the club was one slight mistake. You were inebriated and, false modesty aside, I have that effect on women. But seeing you on the stage yesterday scrambled my mind. I needed to find you, I needed to be close to you, and the connection drew me in. I only planned to tell you how amazing you were but finding you still dressed like that, and willing — my impulses got the best of me and by the time I realised what I was doing, I had you splayed open for me and —" he stopped, taking a deep breath in and I giggled proudly.

Then I didn't.

"So you thought I was your daughter and you shoved your tongue down my throat and grabbed my ass like a lifejacket? Oh...you are a creep..." I whispered slowly.

He cringed. "I didn't know. You don't understand the surge of energy, the calling I felt..." he tried to explain, but reason stopped him. "It never happened with Anwen," he confessed. "She is a beautiful woman, yet the only thing I feel towards her is just that, that she is of me, that my power belongs in her."

"That still sounds creepy and highly sexual, Rhy," I exclaimed, unable to stop my thoughts. This was some very messed up Game of Thrones situation.

"No, no, it's different," he raised his hands and flicked his fingers in frustration. "You don't understand, the type of energy that calls me to you differs from what I feel towards Anwen. Or Erik. Which is why I spoke to her this morning, and as soon as she told me you two are not blood related, it all made sense!"

"What made sense?" I frowned.

"You and me. The calling I feel towards you. If you allow me sunshine, I shall very much like to listen to it."

Day 8

The bed felt so cosy, like a cloud hugging me tightly, the warmth emanating from the duvet enveloping my senses. I opened my eyes to see the city lights and the night sky and smiled to myself, knowing that I still had a long way till morning and I could enjoy a few more hours of sleep.

An arm wrapped tighter around me, sensing that I had awoken, and pulled me closer, pinning my back against more warmth. Mmm...it felt nice. It also felt human. What the…?

I turned abruptly to find Rhylan splayed next to me, shirtless and without pants, one of his bare legs wrapped tightly around my own while his arm draped around my torso. What time was it? How did we get here?

I vaguely remembered Rhy ordering pizza, which we ate in a long silence while I processed everything he told me and once we got to dessert, a vegan chocolate brownie he ordered along with the pizza, I started raising a few questions of my own.

The first obvious one was how in the hell did he know my address and how had he dared to order food, which conveniently arrived at about half two, just as he splayed the big news on me. Then I went into more pressing and important matters. What did he want with Anwen? Was Ansgar truly alive and why was he causing so much pain to his own daughter?

It felt weird in my mouth to even say it. Anwen was Rhy's daughter. I was touched all over by Anwen's father. Yuk, yukkity yuk.

No matter how much I tried to reason with my brain and still had very fuzzy feelings whenever Rhy looked at me, as soon as I said or thought about the relationship, things started to get weird. This still felt like a Game of Thrones situation to me. I mean, I wouldn't mind turning into a badass like the characters, but it all had a creepy vibe. Can we just make it the word of the day?

He answered uncomfortably, bearing the heaviness of my judgement and refused to reveal his plans because apparently, they were still forming and could change within the second. The gist was that yes, Ansgar was still alive, not in the best shape, since he was held by an enemy kingdom, but faeries had quick regenerating capabilities. When I questioned that, instead of explaining it to me, he simply took a knife and slashed his arm, letting dark blood drip all over my fluffy carpet.

"Thanks for that, now I have to invent a story for the dry cleaner's that doesn't involve a murder scene," I grimaced and threw a pillow in his direction. By the time he threw it back, the wound had evaporated. Along with the blood from my carpet. At least that sorted a problem.

"I am the last direct descendant of the god. I am made entirely of his energy," he said with a tilt of his head, like that was supposed to mean something to me. I cannot leave it behind. It returns to me unless I willingly pass it on. It works the same with the goddess' energies, which is why they cannot be stolen."

"So, if you are decapitated, will your head follow along?" That was a gruesome image and my mind flew to the head on a tray from Tim Burton movies.

Rhy chuckled. "First it will fade, along with my body, which means I will momentarily be dead. Then, once all energy is absorbed back, I will be reformed."

"Ew…" But then I thought better of it. "Where do you go when you are dead? I assume heaven is not an option for mass murderers?" I cringed at my own words.

"Where do you go when you dream?" he retorted.

"I don't, I'm still there," I replied with confusion and he nodded.

"Same, even though I no longer hold possession of my body, I still exist. And then I awake again."

"Huh…" I focused on finishing the rest of the brownie. Even though my stomach already told me *no* a couple of times, I continued to shove food down my throat to avoid my brain from spinning so hard. I didn't know if it was effective or not, because that's the last thing I remembered. I finished the brownie, then found a couple of pillows to make myself more comfortable after such a big meal and then here I was, cuddling with a killer faerie that happened to be my sister's dad. Which made calling him 'daddy' permanently out of the question!

I took the time to watch him for a while, enjoying how the moon coloured different shapes on his cheek and was surprised to discover the amount of tattoos his body possessed with such intricate designs. They adorned his neck, both of his arms and torso, lowering down his back with a weaving of secrets, branded forever into his skin.

I did not know what they meant. Some of them had stories and quotes, while others described symbols I had not seen before. Enchanted by the closeness and this unfamiliar sight of him, I took a long while to scan his body.

I never noticed how long his eyelashes really were, but right now, I admired their eagerness to fan across his under eye. I would kill for natural lashes like that.

Something about seeing him rest, looking at him being truly relaxed, made me want to nestle myself into him again and enjoy him like that, carefree, as if all that heaviness he had to carry over his shoulders every day finally dissipated. His lips were slightly curved, like he was having a really good dream.

What am I to do with you? I observed him for a while longer, my hands shaking with the need to touch and enjoy those perfectly sculpted muscles, trying to form some kind of plan yet, managing to do nothing but watch him sleep. He was truly a beautiful man, having that sort of beauty that would last through centuries, universal and unequal.

I turned slowly to check my phone. 2:33 am. Yeah, we had a long way till morning. I didn't feel like sleeping again. If my assumptions were correct, I'd probably fallen asleep right after eating and seeing how the night before I'd attended a party and an early morning radio show, missing sleep had taken its toll.

Which also meant that Rhylan babysat my sleepy ass and

randomly decided to join me, wearing only his underwear. I turned towards the other nightstand, one that only held a lamp because no one had slept here since Erik last visited, to see that he had claimed ownership of the space and placed his watch, wallet and phone there, like it was the most normal thing to do before getting into bed with a passed out woman.

His phone! He left his phone. I turned slowly, careful not to rock the bed too hard, and reached over, causing his arm to squeeze me harder and bring me closer to him. I almost dropped the phone on his head from the sensation, his skin on mine and the warmth he sent all over my body, especially in some places I was not ready to admit.

I turned quickly and tapped on the screen, praying to everyone who would listen not to find a password. It opened with a standard background and went straight into the menu. No codes required.

Yes, yes, yes, come to mama.

The first thing I did was to decrease the brightness as low as it could go to avoid the screen light from breaking his sleep, then debated whether to start with WhatsApp or emails. The choice was made for me because he had no WhatsApp messages whatsoever.

Half an hour later, I got bored with finding only business reports and emails confirming stock purchases and sales.

Boring, boring, boring. I tried to see if he'd logged in with another email but rhylan.gordon was the only one he seemed to have.

I tried Facebook to find no account had been created. Same with Instagram. He didn't have Tiktok installed and honestly, I wouldn't really picture him a dance for people kind of guy.

So I was only left with the text messages and recent calls. I went into call history first to see my name, then Anwen, Jason and Elsa and somebody named Tony Millian. No other calls. Maybe he had just gotten this phone, because nothing lasted longer than ten days.

Text messages didn't reveal much either, the same names again. I didn't go into any of the messages he had exchanged with Anwen or the Odstars because, even though I was spying on him, it felt too invasive, even for me. Then he had our messages, and I could not help but smile with pride when I spotted the little star that marked my name as favourite and saved our conversation on top of all the others. Then this Tony guy, who seemed to be some kind of employee because all texts were business related and someone else named Mark.

Into Mark it is.

Rhylan: I need you to do some research for me. It's urgent.

Mark: Yes, boss

Rhylan: As soon as you get the info, you are to burn it and erase it from memory. Is that clear?

Mark: Of course boss

Rhylan: I need the address for Cressida Thompson, lives in NYC

Two hours later, Mark responded.

Mark: Three Cressida Thompson in NYC boss, one lives in Hudson Yards, one in East Village and one in Astoria.

Rhylan: How am I supposed to know? Beautiful blonde woman, stunning blue eyes, 5 feet four

Rhylan: Try Odstar, she might have changed her name

Mark: Influencer Cressida Thompson?

Rhylan: Yes

Mark: Use the address in Hudson Yards boss

Rhylan: Security?

Mark: Guard change is at eleven PM. I'll text you an imprint for the elevator code. Penthouse 3.

The messages ended without Rhylan texting a thank you and restarted today at 1:27AM.

Rhylan: Another job for you

Rhylan: Get me one of these and have it delivered to the address you gave me. I need it first thing in the morning.

The last thing I expected was to see a photo of dad's Remy

bottle, which Rhylan seemed to want to have replaced. I sighed. It was not about the bottle, but the fact that it was one of dad's most prized possessions and one of the few things I had brought with me from the old house. Still, I appreciated the thought, no matter how weird this spy business was. I will have to sleep with a baseball bat by my side for the rest of my life and have the locks changed first thing tomorrow.

Mark: Boss, that's gonna be a hard one

Rhylan: Which is why you are paid ten times your rate to get it done. Add yellow roses, as many as the florist can give, search for the nicest kind. And champagne. Make it impressive.

Mark: Rosé or white?

Rhylan: What?

Mark: Rosé or white for the champagne.

Rhylan: Rosé

Mark: 1996 Dom?

Rhylan: Yeah, whatever, get me a dozen of those as well.

Rhylan: And make a donation to a whale protection foundation and get me a big thank you check for that. Under the name Cressida Thompson.

Mark: Messed it up that bad, boss?

Rhylan: Shut the fuck up and do as you're told

I threw the phone away after that, my heart racing a

thousand miles per hour. Did Rhylan care that bad about my tiny breakdown from the day before that he was willing to spend money just to get back on my good side?

He had some guy hack into my life, then used the same guy to order this huge gesture, asking him to manage the impossible in a day. Even Amazon Prime would be jealous. Part of me wanted to freak out at him right now and kick him out, and the other part didn't want to ruin the surprise. Was it so bad that even knowing how weird this all was, I wanted to enjoy myself? That I loved being cuddled by Rhylan and loved having him sleep in my bed like we were a well-established couple?

I had so many more questions, yet none of the answers seemed important, not while I looked at him to see him peaceful like that, not when I would crumble his entire happiness by waking him up.

Was I a bad person? Was I betraying my friend?

An hour later, I rested the phone back on the nightstand, eliminated all traces of my intrusion and laid on the pillow, shimming back inside Rhy's embrace.

After all, why should the whales suffer?

I woke up at ten, alone in my bed. No sight of Rhylan. The pizza boxes had disappeared, along with the chocolate marks from the bedsheet, all of it replaced with a card that rested on the fluffed up pillow where Rhylan slept the night before.

The same cursive writing, which I immediately recognised.

Please forgive me, sunshine. I would never do anything to upset you. I know it will never compensate for what I did, but there is a surprise for you in the living room.

R

I rushed to the living room, hoping to find Rhylan there. Instead I felt like I'd just stepped into a fairy tale wedding, because my entire apartment was filled with yellow roses. They hung from the walls, leaned from hundreds of vases and occupied so much space that I barely had enough room to make a pathway from the hallway into the living room, where the entire surface of my floor was filled with more roses.

On the table, a crate of champagne rested along with a tall crystal glass with another note underneath.

A place fit for a goddess.
Please enjoy

And on the armchair, right where I'd found him yesterday, was a blue velvet box. I knew exactly what I would find inside, so I was more concerned with the note attached to it.

If you can forgive me, I would love to take you out for lunch tomorrow.
Please call me as soon as you find it in your heart, this fool has waited centuries to find you and waiting for your forgiveness will feel like an eternity.

Inside the envelope was a cheque for one million US dollars, just like he had requested, donated to *Whale and Dolphin Conservation* under my name.

Day 9

"Miss Thompson, Mr Gordon is here for you, and he is insisting that we call to let you know," Alex's weary voice sounded through the phone."

"Yes, tell him I'm on my way," I replied with excitement.

I had probably never gone down as quickly as I did that day, forgetting my lipstick and my emergency charger and choosing flats over high heels. The thought of seeing Rhylan again raised tingles all over my skin and I did not want to prolong the wait, so I practically jumped in the elevator that took me to him.

A minute later, the silver door opened to reveal a very sexy Rhy — like that was any news — along with a super uncomfortable usher who kept looking at the man like he would grow another head and eat him. Which, come to think of it...

"Hello, sunshine," the faerie straightened at the sight of me, extending his shoulders wider, a gesture that made my heart race, if it wasn't already. Whoever made this man, had made him with the sole purpose of torturing women, because he was so beautiful it was painful to look at.

One of my favourite things to watch on YouTube were people's emotional reactions to songs, art, old ladies that had dreamt about seeing a painting in real life and their raw reaction had gained millions of watchers. And right now, seeing Rhylan, I completely understood what being overwhelmed by such artistry meant. And the way he smiled at me, truly smiled. Not one of those short and curt curves of his lips he made when he had to make himself polite, but a true one, one that brought light into his adamant eyes.

"I am starving," I replied as a greeting and licked my lips, which proved to be the wrong thing to do, because his gaze turned ravenous as he took a step forth and leaned into my ear to say, "Me too, sunshine, there isn't a part of you I cannot wait to taste."

Okay... release all the shivers in the world in three...two...one...

And they were good ones, which followed me all the way to the car, that apparently become his to use whenever he needed to and spiked at different moments, making me unable to pronounce a single intelligent sentence. Like when he opened the door for me and caught my hand in his while I settled myself, then when he started driving and stopped at a traffic light and reached for my other hand to place a few gentle kisses over my knuckles and all the glances he threw me whenever traffic allowed. He looked at me with hunger, like I was the last chocolate cake on earth and he was a sugar addict.

Luckily, my heart was in good health because if not, I doubted I would have been able to reach the restaurant from all the palpitations and stomach fluttering every single gaze and contact of our skin brought to me.

"Mister Gordon, just on time," the restaurant manager arrived to greet us as soon as we parked and escorted us to our table, murmuring to Rhy how everything was ready as per his request.

Rhy nodded and thanked the man, then flipped a few notes into his hands when he thought I wasn't paying attention and gently placed his hand on my lower back to help escort me through the tables.

"Rhy, what is this?" I asked in shock as soon as big doors to what looked to be a private room were opened for us to reveal another tonne of yellow roses arranged in beautiful clusters all across the mirrored wall room and a single table for two at the centre, with an ice bucket and a champagne bottle along with two crystal glasses.

"Lunch, sunshine," he smirked knowingly, then added. "I made it bright for you," he grinned, pleased with my reaction.

So all the roses and the cart of champagne from my home weren't enough?

"What will happen to all these flowers? Are there any yellow roses even left in the city?" I spun to admire the room with curiosity. The amount of selfies I would take in here, if it were up to me. I sighed, thinking about the stunning profile photos I could get out of this.

"What's the matter?" Rhy asked, sensing something was on my mind as soon as the manager left.

"Oh nothing, I'm only thinking about the flowers and taking some photos, no big deal, don't worry about it," I smiled and walked towards the table.

"Where do you want them?" Rhy started taking off his jacket to give him more flexibility in movement and grabbed the phone from his pocket, getting ready for me to pose.

"Don't be silly," I giggled. "I don't want to ruin the moment."

"Cress, this is all for you to do whatever you please with. And if you want to take photos for two hours before they serve our food, you can very well do that." I looked at him with a frown, realising he was totally serious and his phone was in position, probably already snapping a few shots of me.

"Do you mind doing it on my phone?" I asked, careful not to offend him. Come to think of it, it was the easiest way, because I already had set filters. All my edits were easier to handle and I didn't have to threaten to kill him if he wouldn't delete all the unflattering ones.

"Sure," Rhy smiled and took my phone. "Whenever you are ready," he added, and I started taking various poses next to the wall of roses, feeling a bit weird and uncomfortable at first, because here I was, ruining a date with my job, but after realising that Rhy was having fun and grinned from ear to ear, sometimes kissing my hand in a photo or pinching my ass to get a more natural reaction, I relaxed and started to enjoy it myself as well.

Half an hour later, after about five hundred photos and a few IG stories, we finally took a seat at the table where we both enjoyed our champagne.

"Thank you for that." I broke the silence that settled across the table. It felt as though as soon as we finished the photo session, we came back to our normal selves and realised this was our first official date.

Guessing we had finished with the decor, the waiters

brought the appetisers and I couldn't help but notice that Rhy kept meat off his plate this time around.

"Are you turning vegan on me now?" I teased him gently, with the most encouraging tone.

"I thought you wouldn't want beef taste all over your lips," his eyes glanced towards mine and made me shiver all over again. The man had plans.

"I appreciate the thought, but there are still a few more things we need to get through for me to even consider letting you anywhere close to my lips, daddy."

As soon as I said it, my entire face turned red and I wanted to be sick, I felt the words coming out of my mouth and I desperately wanted to shove them back inside and delete them from my vocabulary for the rest of my life. Rhy enjoyed my reaction because he started laughing, clearly having some fun times with the struggles of my poor brain.

"Whatever you wish to ask me, sunshine, I am all yours." Of course, those words came out with an innuendo, so I resumed directing my attention to the plate in front of me and carefully arranged the vegan sour cream sauce over my tomato. It took me another two minutes to calm myself enough to look at him again, only to spot him enjoying his food and looking at me with endearment and no small amount of curiosity.

"What are you looking at?"

He giggled again and sounded like a teenager who had just touched his first boob. "I find it fascinating that you accepted everything I am with absolutely no protest, yet my relationship with your friend stuns you in such a manner."

"Speaking of my best friend," since he brought it up I might as well start with that, "what exactly are your plans with Anwen?"

His eyes shifted slightly, almost unnoticeable were I not drowning in them and nodded. "I understand you are concerned for her, however, as I told you two days ago, she is my child. My only child," he pointed and a small frown deepened, like he regretted it.

"And what's the deal with Erik? Do you really expect us to believe he was killed by a fish? When he died in a hospital in Anwen's arms?" I accused and dropped my fork on the plate with a little too much noise.

"Erik's situation is regrettable, believe me I would have wanted him to be the one I pass my powers to. Alas, I was not involved in the siren's plans nor found out about them until it was too late," Rhylan finished with a sip from his glass.

"And mermaids exist and they kill people?" I whispered under my breath. We were alone in a private room and the waiters were by the door. Still, it sounded too crazy, even for me.

"A siren has the ability to shift. You could be one for all I know, were it not for the fact that I kissed you and found out you are not lethal," he tried to explain.

"Not that you know of," I smirked, which made him chuckle again.

"I plan on passing my energy to Anwen, not all of it, just enough to maintain the power of the god. So if you do not believe that I would not harm her, trust that I would not harm myself."

Okay, his argument made a bit of sense, though I was still sceptical about all this faerie business. "And Ansgar?" I pushed.

"What of him?" Rhylan frowned and a wrinkle appeared at the corner of his mouth to mark his distaste for the prince.

"Are you setting him free?" I asked.

"That depends on him, which is a decision out of my control. I also have someone to give answers to and although it looks like I am in control of the world, I am being controlled as well," he admitted and I didn't expect him to tell me that, to reveal his weaknesses.

"Are you talking about your king?"

He huffed below his breath. "I am talking about the queen. She is also a direct descendant of Belgarath, which makes her my equal. Yet, since she is also a queen, I am sworn into her loyalty, which makes her hold certain power over me. Hurting her would mean hurting my own god, my own essence. I could not hold it inside myself for long, thus some of the energy would be lost, forcing a part of my god to vanish."

"Why is it so important to you what a god thinks? He is long dead anyway," I asked, but we were interrupted by the serving of the main course, which we both received thankful and dived right into the deliciousness before Rhy spoke again.

"I assume by now you have become acquainted with our story," he spoke as soon as the last piece of cabbage roll disappeared from his mouth. I nodded and continued enjoying my own.

"When he was entombed, the god made a last creation, his last wish. He threw his power into the ground and created the firelings, beings designed to take over the other kingdoms and avenge his perish. When he died, when he truly vanished, one last tear fell from him. His essence, the last drop of energy after millennia of suffering. Which is how my bloodline came to be." He stopped and analysed my features for a while, making sure that I was following.

"And what is the main goal?" I skipped the dramatics of how the faeries had suffered wars and rivalries and so on. I didn't enjoy history all that much.

"To bring our god back and enable him to finish what he started," he admitted.

"Which is?" I questioned with another frown.

"The beginning. We were all born of it, and we must return to it. All there is, all that you see, needs to change. That is how it was always meant to be, before the goddesses ruined creation. The god would have listened, he would have reasoned, if the time was right, but now it must all be delivered back to its original state. There were too many shifts in power after his departure."

And that's when I finally saw Rhylan for what he was. What all the internet articles spoke of, what Anwen had tried to make me see. He was the devil. Or well, what we thought the devil would be like. Here to kill us all.

His lips shook while his eyes remained pinned on me, scanning my every reaction and I noticed that his fingers, although gripping the glass tight enough to make his fingertips white, trembled slightly over the crystal.

"Why are you not scared?" he finally questioned.

"I understand your reasons. I do not approve, I don't think that everyone should die or that one person should have power over the majority. Although yes, I agree that creation, and by it I mean humans, has gone out of control."

He looked at me with surprise, so I continued. "Honestly, if you, your god or whomever don't kill us, we'll do it ourselves in about fifty years or so." I raised my shoulders, knowing it was something inevitable with the way the planet was suffering.

Abruptly, Rhy relaxed in his seat and expelled a breath he must have held for a very long time, because after the air came out of his lungs he looked like a different person. Younger, relieved. "You are the first human to ever tell me this. In my entire existence," he admitted.

"Well," I tilted my head because I honestly didn't know if it was meant as a compliment or not. "I'm realistic. I've seen a lot of shit in my life and I don't agree with most of the rules."

Seeing how he didn't move in his seat and was paralysed while listening to my words, I continued. "I am lucky to be born in a Western country, but say I hadn't been this lucky and I was born in a country where I'd be starving by the age of three. Or be forced to marry at the age of twelve and considered a middle-aged woman by now. Or god forbid, in a country that wouldn't give me a right to vote or to do what I will with my body. The world is terrible, meant only for people with money and power to enjoy it."

There was so much more I could do, so much I could invest in to help others and even though I donated fifty percent of my profits every year, it was still not enough. And I knew it. I did not have the time to criticise myself further, because Rhylan's lips engulfed mine, kissing me like I had just returned breath into his life.

Day 10

Everything changed after the kiss that escaped from Rhy's lips like a vow. It made him overthrow everything he wanted and all that he had planned and let himself enjoy the freedom of his impulses. We devoured each other's lips with an obsessive grip, both of us struggling to let go, even during the much needed times when we had to take a breath. We fed from one another's mouth with desperation, clawing onto that connection none of us had felt before, the perfect synchrony of our minds and bodies coming together.

And we continued to do so for the rest of the afternoon, during which Rhy barely unpegged his mouth from mine, enough to bring us back home. We kissed in the hallway, taking small steps and blindly pushing each other towards the elevator and all the way to my apartment without giving a damn who was watching us. I threw him on the couch and spread my legs to cover each side of his hips and continued devouring those lips, that neck and bit down all the way to his shoulders until the moon rose in the night sky.

The attraction I felt for the man was insane, so much that my body jolted with his every touch and caress. I wanted to move us into the bedroom and started pulling at his shirt with visible determination, but his hands caught my palms every time and only stopped paying attention to my mouth to place a few kisses to my eager fingers.

"Let me enjoy you slowly," he pleaded and one gaze from those glazy dark eyes made me shiver enough to agree to everything he wanted.

Which brought us here, with an hour left in the movie and Rhy's hand slowly caressing the inside of my thigh. When he left my home the previous night, he asked if he could accompany me wherever I had planned to go the following day, which happened to be a movie premier of a good friend of mine. I had spent most of the day in my friend's company, helping her with gown suggestions and taking advantage of her hair and makeup team and only met Rhy again on the red carpet, where he waited quite a while by the photographer's area until he spotted and joined me.

Throughout the day, Anwen texted and called as well, she could not attend the event and wished our common friend Mikah the best and we chatted for a while. She asked me about Rhy and how things were going, concerned that he was taking too much of my time and she did not want to interfere with any plans, so I kept things vague and told her that yeah, I was seeing him quite a lot but things were uneventful and fairly boring.

To my surprise, Anwen was relieved rather than worried, which made me feel awful for keeping the truth away from her. Even if I wanted to spill the beans and warn her about what was to come, I had little to no information on Rhy's kingdom and his powers. All the complicated energy binding he had tried to explain washed over me at the sight of his mouth, moving in such a teasing way.

By the time I hooked myself to his arm, I realised how well we fitted together. I had chosen a golden gown with various skirt lengths which made the train of the dress look puffy and grunge, while he opted for a classic tux, relaxing his appearance with a black shirt, unbuttoned at the neck.

Together, we were a sight to behold and I finally understood why he called me 'sunshine', when I took a celebratory selfie in the mirrored displays. We were like night and day, darkness and light coming together. His dark ebony hair and those piercing onyx eyes, along with the black outfits he displayed most of the time, clashing against wavy blonde hair and fair skin, with golden or yellow gowns. Do I need to say that I broke the internet by posting a runway photo with Rhylan or is that already understood?

After we walked inside and I introduced him to my friends, we were escorted to our seats and offered champagne, which we both gladly accepted and started enjoying the film. Rhy's fingers interlocked with mine and he rested his hand on my leg, while keeping my palm on top of his like a prised possession. When I let go to reach for another glass of champagne, it started moving on his own accord, teasing my knee and now, the inside of my thigh.

I enjoyed the way his skin trailed on mine, yet after a couple of seconds I realised that the ascent did not plan on stopping, so I placed my hand over his and threw him a quick questioning glance, trying not to make it too obvious to the couple sitting next to us. When my eyes reached Rhylan's face, wickedness lined his features and his eyes became the most obscure black I'd ever seen.

"Keep watching the movie, your friend is in this scene," he murmured into my ear as he released the words, so softly that they had their own touch as they fell on my neck. I swallowed a lump in my throat and pointed my gaze to the screen, placing both my arms together over my lap and releasing his hand, a silent approval to continue what it had planned.

A slow groan escaped Rhy's throat, delight overpowering him at the newly gained freedom and with a single flowing movement, he grabbed the train of my dress and placed it on top of my own hands, covering my pelvis entirely, leaving exposed only the leg he had begun to have fun with.

I exhaled slowly, wondering what would happen and curious enough to let it flow, so as soon as Rhy's fingers began trailing upward again, I relaxed my muscles and allowed him to slowly, barely noticeable, climb towards my upper thigh. Where, of course, he did not stop, using his pointer finger to flick my panties to the side in an abrupt slide, leaving me completely and utterly exposed, where it not for the waves of organza cuddled into my lap.

"What are you doing?" I whispered, keeping my eyes hooked to the screen. I only heard a low murmur, the faerie shushing me, his sole attention hanging on that finger.

Of course it was not enough to tempt me with just a flick of his finger and the terror of the theatre lights suddenly scanning us for everyone to see because he added another one, playing with my folds with the amazement of a teenager slipping into pussy for the first time. The first brush of his touch was soft, exploratory, allowing me to get used to the calluses millennia of loneliness had created. Once he became confident that my introduction had long been accomplished. Rhy started moving them around, dragging those damned fingers up and down, up and down, in a torturously pleasant rhythm that made my stomach drop and my pelvis jitter.

God, the way he knew how to touch me, how to play with my body, and he hadn't even reached my clit yet. This man was pure desire and had been around for a really long time, which meant that he clearly knew how to satisfy a woman. As a response to my thoughts, his thumb made an appearance and did I just say he hadn't paid attention to my clit? Let's just scratch that because the way he touched me to create the perfect amount of pressure at the first contact had me rise from my seat a few inches from the dip of pleasure.

"Shhh.." Rhy whispered into my ear again as he tilted his body slowly towards mine, like he just had a thought about a scene and he couldn't wait to share it with me. "Keep watching the screen, sunshine," he murmured with a roughened voice, while his hand cupped my pussy and those two fingers that had nonchalantly played on the sides had now become the centre of attention, since they abruptly penetrated inside of me, his thumb making lazy circles on my clit.

Oh my god, can I just die now! The way he moved, the

way he expertly worked me from inside and out at the same time, made me want to jump out of my skin with sensation, with pure joy. I was so full of him, those two damned fingers reached so deep inside of me, perfectly aligning with my outer pleasure and after a couple of seconds, during which he had shown mercy and let me adapt, he started moving demonically, my entire existence becoming reduced to the feeling, to the insatious amount of pleasure I was given and how my body did not know how to absorb it.

"Rhy…" I whispered, warning him, though all that came out was a slow whimper, which made the man mad with urgency, wanting to squeeze all my juices.

I tried to breathe; even my lungs didn't know how to process so much pleasure. I needed to scream, to claw at him, to spread my legs wider and take him in, to release all the sensation somehow, but I could only bite my lips and hold it in, abruptly aware that another man was seated right next to us.

"Rhylan, stop," I tried to beg. Still, my lips did not utter the words properly, sounding like tiny screeches rather than the request of a determined woman. I turned to see his eyes fixated on me, wide and aware, focus and excitement flicking in his gaze.

"The screen," he ordered, and I had no other choice but to

do just that, while his hand raised my pelvis just an inch or two above the seat to give him better access inside of me.

Oh, my god I was going to…"Rhylan!" I shrieked, my nails jabbing at his hand, trying to make it stop, trying to halt the sensation, to no avail.

Rhy focused only on me, only at the place where his fingers met my soft insides and pumped desperately into me while his thumb flicked my clit like it was a PlayStation button and he was at the last monster before finishing the game.

I gripped the edge of my seat and drew a sharp breath, preparing myself for what was to come and in the next second, wave after wave of pleasure extended all over my body, to the point that I almost wanted to faint from the overwhelming satisfaction. I probably squealed a few times, but it all came muffled and only when I relaxed enough to sit on my chair again without whimpering did Rhy retract the fingers that had brought me such sweet torture.

Pleased with the results, he threw the train of my dress back to the floor and situated himself in the centre of his seat, continuing to watch the movie as if nothing had happened. It was only when I tilted my gaze towards him that I spotted him slowly licking his fingers, the same ones that had been inside of me, enjoying every bit of my taste. The sight drove me mad.

After the movie ended, we both rose from our seats and clapped eagerly, even though at this point neither of us had any idea what the plot had been about. We lingered for an hour or two at the after party, congratulating Mikah for her stunning interpretation and chatting away with the rest of the cast and other celebrities.

I noticed the ire in some of the women's eyes when spotting Rhylan next to me, though, as opposed to that first night, I did not think it funny anymore and returned them an abrupt gaze that said something along the lines *Bitch, he's mine*.

When it was time to leave the event, considering how both of us had quite a lot to drink, Rhy made a call and within five minutes, a black car arrived to pick us up. I didn't have time to study the make, nor did I really care, since all I wanted was to be next to this man again and kiss the heck out of him. I still didn't know if I was grateful for the earth shattering orgasm or if I hated him for doing that to me, so I kept my kissing rough and involved a lot of biting, just to relay both of those messages.

I did not know how long we'd been kissing for because the car had been parked for a while in front of my building by the time I unhooked my lips from his and he did the same with his hands from my ass.

Always the gentleman, Rhy got out of the car first and rushed to open the door for me, extending a hand to help me up, which I eagerly took and placed another quick kiss on his lips as I stood.

"Do you want to come up?" I murmured, afraid to look at him and face rejection.

"I shouldn't," he said and planted another kiss on my fingertips.

Of course he is not coming. He has better things to do than waste his night with you, my inner self reprimanded my silly thoughts.

"Good night," I forced a smile and hurried to the stairs and through the entry door before he had a chance to reply.

Watching the elevator screen, I realised he had brought me home at twelve o'clock sharp. The perfect gentleman.

Day 11

I opened my door and was greeted by the thousands of roses, still in full bloom, shining in the moonlight along with a figure lurking in the darkness.

My heart jolted, terror paralysing my muscles until Rhylan stepped closer to the hallway light, enough for me to recognise him.

"You said you didn't want to come up," I whispered, noticing that his jacket had disappeared and his shirt was unbuttoned lower than it had been a minute ago, displaying all those tattoos I hadn't had a chance to inspect up close until now.

"I said I shouldn't, not that I wouldn't," Rhy responded before his body pinned me to the wall.

His gaze became ferocious as he took me in, desperately

inhaling the air I let out before he spoke again. "Let me make you glow, sunshine." A promise, one I did not come to understand until later on.

His lips clashed with mine, a hungry and eager encounter. It had been minutes since they'd joined. As soon as my tongue struck his, I relished in the familiar taste, his mouth offering a welcoming sensation.

Rhy's hands wandered across my body, touching me in places he had not allowed himself to do so until tonight, so I could not help but do the same. Leaving all bashfulness behind, I reached in between his legs, hoping to find traces of desire, and I almost jumped at the sizable bulge I'd found there, tensing the fabric of his pants almost to the point of ripping through.

For the first time since I'd met him, Rhy moaned under my touch and the sound protruded more exquisitely than anything I'd imagined. His head dropped back, allowing his chin to align with the ground as he let himself go, enjoying the touch of my hands and the contact he had not let me feel before then.

"One word, Cressida and I'll stop, but you need to speak it now," his gaze darted towards mine again, allowing me to spot a flicker that had not been there before. A new part of him, a caged monster, waiting to break free. I understood the request, what he meant to say. If I wanted to stop this, it needed to be right away, because as soon as he unleashed himself, there would be no turning back.

For a second, hesitation overpowered me. Was I really doing this? Was I prepared to have sex with a thousand old immortal man who looked so good every single woman on earth wanted to take a bite? More importantly, would I be able to control whatever happened after this?

My insides told me that yes. Yes, I was. No matter what I had to do, say or live through to get that thing from his pants free and inside of me, it was a hard yes. Hard indeed, I thought as I gripped it again, eliciting another sound from the immortal man. A sound that signed my undoing.

"What are you waiting for?" I squeezed his crotch for emphasis, a silent demand to take those pants off already and with a very satisfied grin, he did just that. Boxers fell down a second after his pants and, for full disclosure, Rhy ripped his own shirt, making the tiny buttons spring all across the hallway, leaving himself bare to me.

My mouth watered at the sight of him, and I almost wanted to fall to the floor. He was so beautiful it was vulgar, so much perfection added into a single human. Well, not human, I reminded myself.

The faerie took a step back, then another, displaying

himself to me fully, and I had to control the urge to ask him to spin for me, because I wanted to have a look at what I would assume would be a perfect ass. After all, it had to match the rest of his god-like body.

Apart from the eternal beauty on his face, which we had already established, the rest of his body was sculpted like a marble statue, copying one of the masterpieces that belonged at the Louvre. Intricate tattoos draped swirls across both of his arms, covering him in black and grey sleeves and joined on his shoulder blades, to then lower on his chest.

I made a mental note to admire the art once all this was through, although we had a long while till then. His bare chest allowed the eyes to get accustomed to untouched skin, to then lead to his abdomen which was in itself an anatomy lesson. Even those pelvic muscles were just tight enough to point to the best part of him.

I needed to draw in a breath in order to admire the in between his legs as it deserved properly, because my oh my, that dick was made to bring pleasure. My mouth instantly watered, and I had very vivid visions of where it would go and all the things I wanted to do to it. Rhylan must have noticed my lingering eyes because another smirk cropped up on his face, daring me to do just that.

"Okay, pretty boy, my turn." I regretted not going for that

last glass of champagne because I felt like another drop of liquid courage was needed as I unzipped my dress and let it slide down my hips to show my breasts and thong, which I then removed slowly, pinning his gaze as his eyes wandered across my body, widening with the discovery of each part.

When my panties came down, his cock greeted my newly revealed skin with a twitch. It was like our members already knew what to do and were trying to push us into each other, eager to start. Rhy and I took another few seconds to admire one another, that intimacy and truth we were both willing to share. The part that had united us since the beginning.

"You are exquisite," Rhy was the first to break the silence and with it, he took a step towards me, reclaiming part of the territory.

My skin vibrated at his closeness, ready to embed itself all across his body, yet, before I had a chance to move, the immortal faerie fell to his knees in front of me, his head perfectly aligned with my pelvis.

"What are you doing?" Was this really the best time for prayer, or was this some kind of ritual he needed to perform?

My frown disappeared as soon as his tongue revealed his intentions and to make it clearer, he confirmed my suspicion.

"I'm doing what one is supposed to do when in front of a goddess. Worshipping you."

And with it, Rhylan's mouth lunged towards my pelvis and in between my thighs, eager to re-encounter the taste he had enjoyed earlier this evening.

His tongue swum between my legs, rejoicing at the newly claimed territory and I almost fell to the ground were it not for his hands cupping my rear and sustaining my weight while his head pushed forwards to spread my legs wider to receive him. His chin pinned onto my folds as his tongue swept through me and inside of me, the man feasting like he hadn't eaten in a century and I was just what he needed to recover his strength.

I did not last long, not after what he had done to me during the movie and in a matter of minutes I released waves of pleasure onto his tongue, which he gladly absorbed and sucked from within me, stroking me until he left me fully empty and sated.

Only then did Rhy raise his gaze, a silent request to continue claiming me and before I even had a chance to nod, I found myself swept into his arms and carried to the bedroom, where he laid me on top of the covers with unexpected gentleness.

I remained there, panting and begging for him and luckily, he listened because once he quickly scanned my body to make sure everything was alright; he jerked a knee to separate my legs and sheath his body in between my hips, his hardness aligning with my entrance.

"Do it," he murmured, eyes pinning me under him, scanning my face and my hair? His eyes darted somewhere around me and whatever he spotted made him draw in a breath, shifting his gaze back at me to say those words again. "Please…"

I did not know what he was asking for and I did not care because the need for him, to feel him inside of me and discover what that length and girth would do to my body was the only thing I cared in that moment, so, without averting my eyes from his, I reached in between us to the spot where he poked at my pelvis and grabbed him, stroking a few times just in case. Judging by the hardness, he did not need any more preparation.

With this, I placed the tip of him at my entrance and, since he made absolutely no gesture and looked at me with a stunned gaze, I pushed my hips lower into it, just enough to open myself and receive an inch of him inside, paving the way for his thrusts.

"Cressida, please," he echoed and his eyes looked demonic, trapped in some kind of trance and painful torture because, suddenly, his entire body started shaking.

"What? Do you not like it?" I frowned, not understanding this man. First he had finger-fucked me and then ate me like there was no tomorrow and now he just froze on top of me and looked at me like he was a thousand year old virgin.

"I love it, but please, stop torturing me. I cannot take it, not now." I watched how the muscles of his shoulders shook, how his abdomen shivered and his dick twitched, all signs pointing at how much he wanted this, yet there he stood, dumbfounded at my entrance.

"How am I torturing you?" I rasped at him, suddenly very aware of the weirdness of this situation. Did he not like my boobs or something? Because he seemed thrilled to play with them a minute ago while he was eating me up.

"Cressida," he said my name in between pants, visible struggles of whatever battle happened inside of him lined across the features of his face. "I am not allowed to join with a human without their verbal permission."

"Huh?"

"It's one of our rules," he growled, almost in pain, his eyes pleading.

"What are you—" Then it hit me. Anwen had explained something about faeries not being able to show themselves to humans without consequence, so it must have been one of those things. Which made no sense because Rhy had been more than happy to accompany me everywhere and even posed as a human, had all those businesses and creepy people spying for him. My brain went suddenly numb, because whatever the reason, I really did not want to debate it right now, only giggled at the ridicule of their rules.

"Rhy, will you fuck me, please?" Before the words fully escaped my mouth, the faerie unleashed himself and thrusted into me with all the tension and anxiety I had created, a volcano ready to erupt.

It took him a few seconds of desperately pumping into me, which made my stomach twitch and my insides were forced to split abruptly apart to take him in, until he calmed himself enough to regain his speech.

"By the god woman, I thought you were going to let me die," he exhaled in between strokes, his features turning into relief, allowing pleasure to replace thought.

"I didn't know," I giggled again. "You should have told me." I smiled at him, thinking about the vampires who were not allowed to come inside, and my mind went wild with the word association.

"Is what I do to you a laughing matter?" His dark voice rippled over me and brought me back into my body, a body that was being hammered into.

I pinned my gaze to his and smiled again, making him wonder. If I was to have this man, I would have him whole, full of passion and anger and wrath.

"Let's see if you will laugh after this." Rhy's returned a dark smile, which was the last thing I remember before my body was turned into a sacrificial altar where the faerie brought offerings of pleasure.

He invaded every part of me, treating my vagina like a territory he had made a mission to explore fully because he had gotten himself into angles and corners I did not know existed. He turned and twisted me, each time shoving himself deeper, more brutally, until I did not know what my body would feel like without him stuck inside of me. Needless to say, I had an insane amount of orgasms. At one point I found myself bent over the nightstand with my face stuck to the window while Rhy rammed into me from behind, my sweat and wails of pleasure leaving tiny steams on the glass.

He did not stop even when I started trembling from the effort of producing so much pleasure, when I lost my voice from shouting and acknowledging my orgasms. He did not stop when my head tilted back and I started screaming that I would die right then and there.

Well Cressida, you wanted immortal sex, there you go. Note to self: it might kill you.

I opened my eyes to find Rhy playing with my hair and using it as a brush to make shapes over my left nipple. I turned to him and swallowed dryly.

"Did I die?" I tried to speak, feeling like my voice was barely there.

"Almost," he chuckled. "But I'll keep you alive for a while longer."

"I hate you," I tried to spit the last words before exhaustion claimed me fully.

"You love me," Rhy responded with a content smirk.

I smiled lazily, eyes closing on their own accord, my body shutting down. "Mmm…" I took another breath. "I do…"

Day 12

"Rhylan, it is not humanly possible to have this much sex!" My body was shaking with the array of orgasms it had lived through in such a short span of time and I was in desperate need of another shower because all of me was covered in Rhylan.

"Said the woman who woke me in the middle of the night, asking for more," he released my nipple from his teeth just enough to speak, then returned to the activity he had been engrossed in.

"That was a momentary lapse in judgement," I defended myself and tried to shimmy away from under him, but his elbows shifted to trap me while his pelvis reconnected with mine to pin me once more under the sex-obsessed faerie.

"Which is why you need to accept your punishment," he

groaned as he slipped into me yet again, making my insides throb and my body shiver.

In all fairness, he let me rest for an hour or two after that absurd sex marathon we initially had, so I couldn't complain too much. In fact, I couldn't complain at all because what he had given me was the best sex of my life. Nope, scratch that. The best sex anyone has ever had, ever.

And he proved to be a very generous lover. For some reason, I did not expect that of him. I always pictured bad guys to be selfish and wanting it all for themselves, which he had done so while dominating the hell out of my body those first few hours. After he found pleasure a couple of times and sated his urges, the faerie had become calm and playful.

We experimented with each other's bodies; he made a point to use his tongue and paint a few masterpieces in between my legs and when I wanted to do the same, he stopped me, insisting that we had better things to do and redirected his attention back to me.

And here we were again, joining our bodies in wonder and despair, contorting and clashing into each other like a long awaited victory dance. For some reason, my pussy hated me, but loved Rhylan. Every time I had to pee, she was sore and shouted at me to stop torturing her, yet every time Rhy paid her attention, there she was, forgetting all about her sorrows and jumping to meet him.

"Okay, we really need to stop this," I released the words as soon as Rhy pumped a few more times into me, drawing out his own pleasure.

"Hm... the lady is displeased," he turned to the side and rested his head on my tummy, looking at me with puppy eyes, making me the mean woman who took his cookie away.

"No, do not twist my words, the lady is not displeased, the lady is sore as hell!" I accused and turned to the side, making his head slide away from my abdomen and hurried to the bathroom. As soon as I found myself alone, I locked the door and threw my ass on the toilet, waiting for the pee to arrive and for other things to be released from inside me before I got into the shower.

I didn't check my phone and thought it was already afternoon, since I had a vague memory of wanting to cook breakfast and Rhy bending me over the kitchen counter and having his way with me from behind. Not that I hadn't enjoyed that, but we ended up eating some stale croissants before the party continued on the sofa.

I turned the shower to hot and stepped under the water, allowing it to wash away all the remnants of what my dirty dirty self had done. I probably needed to be washed in holy water to actually clean my skin, because Rhy had explored and enjoyed my body in every single way it was designed to and more.

I shuddered at the thought, the image of his fingers inside my core while he was filling me from behind, the way he played and toyed with my body and those weird shadow thingies that he released when he let himself go made me become liquid all over again.

Apparently, the man had superpowers. He could control and materialise darkness and shadows and use them like his own personal minions. And boy, did he know how to use that power.

"Miss me?" Rhylan appeared by my side in the shower, making me squeal.

"No, no, enough! I can't do this anymore. I will die. Honestly, you will kill me!" I immediately started protesting, although my insides were magically ready for him once more.

"Relax," he chuckled, and that darkness that rippled from his voice... oh my god, this man would literally be the death of me. "Let me help you wash."

Before I had a chance to react or protest, he reached for the sponge and poured body wash over it, flicking it under the water to form bubbles, then he turned me and spread them on my back, rubbing gently.

I let myself fall into that caress, enjoying the way his

calloused fingers trailed over my soft skin, my body recognising the hands that had mapped every inch of me for the past hours.

"What happened here?" Rhy stopped at a point on my lower back, touching the area over and over with the pads of his fingers.

"What?" I turned to find him crouched, his face perfectly level with my ass, gaze pinning that point with intrigue.

"Oh, it's a scar. From when I was little."

"What happened?" he echoed, touching the hard skin.

"I fell over a poker, it was around Christmas and dad had to take a call. I was playing by the tree and then I wasn't, and fell on my ass over the hot poker. They had to rush me to the hospital and everything."

Rhy frowned, and I immediately sensed his thoughts.

"Hey, it was an accident. They were amazing parents," I defended mum and dad.

Rhylan nodded but did not reply, focusing his attention back to my thighs and then my knees, stroking my skin to clean and soothe.

"Why don't you have photos of them? Humans are so obsessed with holding onto memories," he noted and I didn't know if it was directed at me personally, or more of a general observation.

I decided to reply anyway. "I do, but they are at the house. The main house, where we used to live. Haven't set foot in there since I bought the apartment."

"How long ago was that?" Rhy grabbed one of my knees and pulled it slowly, making my leg instinctively turn and take my body around with it. I cannot say I did not enjoy the sight of him kneeling in front of me, all that raw power at my feet, washing the body he had tortured. I felt like Jesus.

"Was Jesus real?" My eyes went wide. I can't believe I didn't even think to ask that before.

Rhy chuckled just as his fingers reached in between my legs through the sponge.

"It's funny how you keep mentioning him. I recall how desperately you shouted his name last night. Funny enough, he was not the one inside you," he pointed out.

"Yeah, I find it weird to scream the name of the guy I'm having sex with, Jesus is a good replacement," I giggled. "Which is still not an answer to my question."

"I don't know," Rhy continued washing my tummy and rose to reach my breasts.

"How can you not know? Couldn't you ask someone? Don't you have like a great-great-grandpa, uncle, cousin, relative of hatred and bloodshed that lived in those times? Aren't you curious?" I recognised, I sounded a bit exasperating but come on. Who wouldn't be curious?

"Why would I be?" Rhy frowned and finished washing my arms, then threw the sponge to the side and reached for the feminine body wash. Okay, this man knew his way around a vagina, I had to give him that. Many women did not even have a clue about ph levels, and here this faerie was, washing in between my legs with the appropriate product.

"He is an invention of the humans, not of my kind, so why would I be interested?" Rhy continued as his fingers traced my folds. "How come you haven't been back to your original house? Do you not miss it?" he changed the subject and I let him. He was obviously uninterested in my questions and clearly upset that I did not think to shout his name in honour of all the waves of pleasure he pinned into me.

"Not really, not anymore at least. I had to leave there in a hurry after the stalker guy," I confessed.

"What stalker guy?" Rhylan stopped abruptly and gazed at me with fire in his eyes, his fingers blocked, cupping my vag.

"Oh, it's an old story. There was this group of men who were obsessed with me, just as I was starting vlogging," I made a gesture to brush my wet hair over my shoulder like I was in *Mean Girls*. "They were local and knew where I lived. Anyway, they came to the house one night to find me.

As soon as I sounded the alarm, they got scared and left. All but one. He attacked me and it was a hard time until the police came." Suddenly, I felt the need to swallow a lump in my throat.

"He attacked you," Rhylan's jaw tightened in such a way that I thought he would break some of his teeth.

"Yeah, he didn't get a chance to rape me because by that time, after what happened at that party I told you about, I became paranoid and had lots of things around to protect myself with."

I gazed at him to find the faerie frozen, absorbing my words with eyes made of pure hatred, so I saw no option but to continue. "When men don't get what they want, they become violent, so... that wasn't fun. I had to have my front teeth replaced," I pointed at the implants with my tongue to show him. No one could notice a difference, but I knew.

"Anwen never told me..." he blinked rapidly, rage flicking into his eyes.

"Oh no, she doesn't know how bad it was. She was in her first year at uni, during finals. The last thing she needed was to find out I was in hospital. Her dad and brother were by my side for three days until I was released, and of course, as soon as the press caught the gist of it, Anwen flew home to be with me. She acted like a mother hen for the following months, I couldn't even pee without her waiting at the door.

"Is that why you don't go there anymore?" he frowned, and did the next logical thing, well... to him apparently, and picked up the shampoo bottle to wash my hair.

"Erik went there to bring me a few things, like my dad's bottle and some of mom's jewellery, and honestly, I do want to go back there, but I just…" I stopped.

He understood my meaning.

"Is there anything you miss from the house in particular?"

"There's this portrait of mum and dad, from their wedding," I confessed. "It hung in my room since I was a baby and when I was old enough, as in probably three, I started questioning my absence from the photo. So one day I grabbed a green marker and climbed on a chair to reach just enough to draw myself at the bottom of the picture. I really wanted to be in it," I chuckled. It must have been one of the first memories I had as a child.

Rhy spun me under the hot steam one last time before he helped me out, taking half a minute to wash quickly while I wrapped myself in towels and as soon as he got out, I passed him one to cover himself with. Not that I minded either way.

Ten minutes later, we got dressed. Rhy had magicked a black shirt and a pair of designer jeans, which got delivered to the door just in time while I chose a maxi dress and let my hair loose to dry naturally.

As soon as I saw Rhy putting his shoes on, I followed and did the same, thinking we were going out to eat since it was late afternoon. When we got to the door, I felt compiled to ask, because I was not wearing makeup — for once — and could not appear at some fancy location in town, to which he casually responded, "we're going to get your picture."

I stopped by the door, frozen. "Excuse me, what?"

"We are going to your old house, so you can get the picture from your room and anything you might want. Just tell me in advance if I need to hire a van."

I blinked in confusion, then looked at him with surprise, tears accumulating at the back of my eyes. What was wrong with me?

Of course I knew what was wrong. He had reached the deepest part of me, my most terrorising fear and here he was, trying to help me overcome it.

"You know I can kill without moving a finger, right?" he tried to encourage me and I had to laugh out loud at the naiveté in his eyes.

"Is that supposed to make me feel better? Knowing I have a serial killer by my side?"

As a response, Rhy reached for my hand and placed a gentle kiss. Only then he lifted his gaze to meet mine. "A serial killer who will defend you with his life."

And just like that, I was liquid again while Rhy nonchalantly opened the door to press the elevator button.

Day 13

"Are you sure you are okay?" Rhylan's voice sounded through the microphone while a concerned beautiful face looked back at me through the screen.

"I'm fine babe, no crying or anything weird, I promise," I said while I forced myself to laugh at the camera.

Little did he know that I'd spent about an hour crying yesterday, something I thought I'd forgotten how to do. As soon as we entered the neighbourhood, my entire body tensed and my mind started getting flooded with memories, ones that I had believed lost forever. As soon as we parked, Rhy allowed me a moment in the car while he made a show of checking the area and ensuring no one was there. I appreciated it, knowing it was solely for the benefit of calming me down, and by the time he returned to the car to get me, I felt ready.

I had to fish out the keys from one of the fingerprint locking compartments the security company added after the incident and passed them to Rhy with shaky hands.

He unlocked the door and studied the hallway, like in one of those police movies. I followed closely, unsure of what I would find, of what feelings might inundate me at the sight of all my abandoned childhood memories, yet the house remained exactly how I remembered it.

I drew a relieved breath as I stepped into the living room, which remained the same, and I almost felt like mom would be just around the corner, bringing cookies from the kitchen while dad sipped whiskey on the sofa, eyes pinned on the news channel.

After a while, the roles had changed and I was the one to lead Rhylan around the house, sharing one story after another about my childhood, about mom and dad or how Anwen and I broke the breastplate of the Malaysian sculpture dad treasured so much and we had to eat three packs of chewing gum to stick it back together. One of the many mischiefs we had slithered through unnoticed.

By the time we got to the bedroom, I'd forgotten about my fear and as soon as I spotted the painting, I ran towards it, my fingers brushing over the colouring I had added as a child.

"Is this it?" Rhy approached me carefully, ensuring I knew it was he stepping into the room. That I was perfectly safe.

"Can't you spot the resemblance?" I chuckled and moved slightly to the side to allow him to see. As soon as his eyes fell on the photo, they gleamed with surprise.

"What?" I frowned, but he stood paralysed, looking at the photo and blinking like an idiot.

"Rhylan, what is it?" I started to get scared.

"I never thought…" he shook his head, refusing to speak.

"What is it?" I raised my voice in desperation.

"I never thought you were so ugly as a child," he admitted, eyes still stuck to the painting and the self-portrait drawn in marker that my three-year-old self must have been very proud of.

And I laughed. I laughed so hard that my voice shook through the walls, awakening the house to its former glory, even just for a second. A house we had lived happily in, where we had shared smiles and jokes and cherished one another. Rhy joined and hugged me from behind, letting himself follow my laughter.

"You look a lot like your mother," he finally said, studying the photo," but you have your father's eyes."

"You would have loved them," I admitted, imagining for

a second what the encounter would have been like.

"Isn't it supposed to be the other way around?" I knew he was frowning from the way he spoke under his breath. "Normally, when a girl brings the boy home for the first time, she tells him not to worry, that her parents are going to love him."

"Oh no, they would have hated you, especially my mom."

"What? Why?" Rhy turned me towards him to check if I was joking. When he spotted my serious face, his eyes flickered with surprise.

"She was very protective of me... and my vajey-jey," I giggled. "She would have hated your guts," I established again, lest there be any confusion.

"Why?" Rhylan pushed again, visibly concerned with this information.

"I mean look at you, you are sex on legs," I pointed the obvious and a satisfied smirk appeared on his face.

After we joked and kissed some more, Rhy helped me pack a few things I wanted to bring back to my apartment, offering like fifty times to come back and bring whatever else I needed.

"Am I really?" Rhy's smiling face from my screen brought me back from yesterday's memories.

"Are you what?"

"Your babe." That smirk again. Things clearly changed between us, and even though neither acknowledged the obvious, having sex with him had completely swapped our stance in the game.

"We'll see..." It was my turn to torture him. "Oh, wear something nice tonight. Extra nice. Jonathan is going to be there." As soon as I said his name, a bitter taste came to the roof of my mouth. I hated the guy. Despised him. While he was with Anwen, he only cared about his job and the business and kept her like a porcelain doll. The sex wasn't very good either, I knew that from the source.

"What is up with this Jonathan? Elsa mentioned him as well."

"He's Anwen's ex. She dated the guy for a while, it got serious, then Erik died and she just went numb. The idiot still hopes to get her back. If you ask me, she made the best decision of her life dumping him. Especially since it led her to Ansgar," I licked my lips as I said his name.

Rhy stopped moving for so long I thought the screen froze. "You met Ansgar?" he finally drew air back into his lungs.

"Not met him, met him. I chatted with him from the cabin. And saw his abs. Uhhh..." I moaned, remembering how sexy the other faerie looked on the sofa next to Anwen that evening when I called.

"Have fun at the party tonight." Rhylan's smile dropped as he spoke the words and ended the call before I could reply.

I had also been invited to this business dinner they all had tonight. Honestly, I would rather shoot myself and secondly, I had to spend the afternoon recording some videos and had a mascara launch that night, so I needed to get ready for a party.

My phone started buzzing while it was pinned to my vanity at five in the afternoon. Rhylan.

"Hey," I planted the camera behind the magnifying mirror, letting him see my face while I worked on my eyebrows.

"Cressida," he said like he didn't expect me to respond.

"Me," I replied, attention fully focused on the pen and drawing perfect lines in between my ingrown hairs.

Ten seconds of silence passed before I checked the screen to see if he was still there. "Everything okay? Is Anwen okay?"

"Yes, she is fine, getting ready, just like you. I think Elsa is making her wear something she doesn't like, so they were arguing over an outfit last time I saw them."

I giggled. "Yeah... Elsa can be... she can be," I only said, keeping the rest of my line of thought to myself.

"Yeah…" Rhy echoed then kept silent again. This time I stopped paying attention to the mirror and pointed my eyes at him.

"What is it?" I was getting worried, because he acted weird. Did something happen?

"Fuck it, I can't do it like this," the faerie said before he disappeared from the screen, letting me see only the wall of his allocated room.

"Rhy?" Before I got an answer, a silhouette formed on the bed, behind me. A cloud of darkness appeared from nowhere, only to materialise into Rhylan, just as I'd seen him a second ago on the screen.

"Oh shit," I exhaled, dropping the pen that fell on the floor with a sharp noise, breaking the glass case.

"Sorry," Rhy apologised with a small grimace, "I'll order you another one, I —"

"It's fine, knowing you, it's gonna be something dramatic, like buying a lifetime supply or hiring the makeup artist. I have a spare one." I dug into my drawer to find the brand new brow liner and pointed it at him.

"Sunshine, we need to talk," he repeated the same words.

Yet again, nothing came out of his mouth.

"So talk," I raised my shoulders in confusion.

He visibly struggled with this and for a highly educated man, who'd been alive since forever, he truly stumbled with the words like a teenage boy.

"I — I have to ask if... I mean I know I shouldn't and I have no right but...I don't think I can—I mean, it's up to you, of course...."

I took pity on him and stood from my vanity to close the distance between us, cupping both sides of his face and raising his chin to me.

"What is it?" I whispered slowly, just like my therapist did when I was getting overwhelmed.

"You are going to a party tonight," Rhy pointed the obvious.

"I am. And you are going to a business dinner."

He nodded, though that was not it, so I pressed for more information. "And?"

He bit his lower lip before he spoke, and I don't think I ever saw him this nervous. "Last time you went to a party... without me..."

I flicked through memories. We'd been to the premiere together, so the last party must have been the fashion show. *The fashion show.* I immediately understood his concern, the obvious manly need to mark his territory. Nevertheless, I also needed him to say it. Why not torture the fae a little, just because I could?

"Yes? I faked confusion.

"You are a free woman, so of course, it is your right to do as you will," he blurted.

"So why are we talking about my party, then?" I released his chin and kept a finger on his jaw, tracing the hard line.

"Cressida, I know this is recent and it may be nothing for you yet, but for me—" he sighed. He actually sighed like an eleven-year-old girl in love with the college student next door.

"Rhy, just spit it out already."

"I'm worried you will find someone else tonight," he confessed. "Someone good."

"And?" I kept playing with his jealousy.

"And you will not want to see me again," his eyes averted from mine in a clear sign of defeat before he continued. "I'm sure Anwen has already filled your head with stories about Ansgar and how amazing, loyal, kind and courageous he is — he stopped to roll his eyes before he spoke again — and all the other qualities the earthlings like bragging so much about," he sighed.

"Of course she has, though what does this have to do with

the party?" Was he really comparing himself to the men I met at parties?

"I know I lack those qualities, and a woman such as yourself might crave for more," he confessed, those dark eyes swirling with defeat.

I frowned. Was that what worried him? That I would randomly meet some new guy?

"I thought it was more to this," I replied earnestly. Here I was expecting the speech 'you are mine, you can't fuck someone else' and all the while Rhy thought I would find something more worthwhile than him.

"There is," he admitted, and I never saw him in that state. His hands trembled in my own and I knew I had the power to ask whatever of him in this exact moment and he would do it. Without a doubt.

"Tell me," I pressed, preparing myself for the claim over my body.

"I'm falling in love with you," Rhylan said instead, his inky eyes looking at me with hope and terror.

Day 14

"Are all descendants such self-entitled bitches or just mine?" Rhylan's voice came through about half a second before his body materialised into my bed. It was eleven in the morning and I was eating toast, planning a full on lazy day.

"What happens if you land on top of me and crush me?" By this point, he had done it three times and I lost the ability to get scared. As soon as shadows started appearing out of nowhere, I knew he would shortly follow.

"I'm able to see the area as soon as my first line of darkness enters the space, so I know where you are. I try to land as closely as possible to you, though," he admitted and lunged for a surprise kiss.

I giggled and passed him the bit of toast I still held, which he bit into eagerly. "Did you skip breakfast?"

He rolled his eyes and released an exasperated sigh. "My blood heir, apart from being an ungrateful bitch, kept me up most of the night. And then had the audacity to hit me!" He raised a finger to make a point, his face red with ire. "As you can imagine, breakfast wasn't at the top of my priority list."

"And what was?" I asked curiously and reached for the last piece of toast, though judging by the way his eyes followed its way to my mouth, I gave up and passed it to him.

"Seeing you, of course," he replied before he took a generous bite.

"So you came to see me to complain about your daughter?" I giggled, imagining the two at each other's throats.

Rhy tsked. "Don't call her that. She is my kin, even though she doesn't deserve it," he groaned before finishing the toast.

"What did you do?" I planted my suspicion on him, which made his forehead wrinkle.

"What makes you think I was the one to do anything?" He tried to defend himself, but I kept my gaze on him and within a few seconds, he started confessing. "We had dinner, and I met Jonathan, who is a prick, you were correct about that."

"Told you," I replied victoriously and started caressing his hair, more by instinct and the need to touch him than anything else. He immediately embraced it and next thing I knew, he planted his head over my thighs and turned to the side to give me better access, while he continued speaking.

Enjoy a free therapy session, why don't you?

"Anyway, he grabbed her on her way out so I—of course — had to step in and we got to chatting as I led her to her door. I pitied her, crying after the princeling, so I allowed them to meet and they fucked. And now she is mad at me," he explained with a tone of voice that clearly stated he had absolutely no idea why my friend was mad.

In all fairness, I didn't either, because he made it sound like a nice gesture. Although, if my sister was mad, she must have had a reason. Especially if she resorted to violence.

"Why do you think she got mad?" I tried a better approach, hoping he would spill the beans.

"Surprisingly, she waited until this morning to raise her hand at me and show how mad she was after she enjoyed a good night of fuckery." Honestly, considering his height, I was surprised that Anwen reached his face properly.

Rhy sighed and nestled more into my touch.

I smiled to myself. I loved seeing him like this, vulnerable and cute, sharing his problems with someone, for once.

"How did they meet? Did Ansgar appear in her bed like you do in mine?"

"No, I copied his energy, blended it with my lines and sent them to Anwen's room," he explained and I blinked for a couple of seconds until it connected, because oh baby Jesus, did I know what Rhy was capable of doing with those 'lines', as he called them. They were basically whiffs of darkness that could materialise all around your body, which the fae had the power to use as his own limbs.

Did I have darkness filling my pussy while Rhylan was filling me from behind? Yes. Did it feel like having two dicks in me at once? Also yes. So I could only imagine what Anwen, my bashful and innocent sister must have been through.

"So you used your darkness and made it seem like her boyfriend had sex with her while you were there watching? Dude, you have some weird kinks!"

"No!" He jumped away from my touch and turned to me, waving his hands in the air as if to remove the idea. "That is disgusting, of course I did not."

"It sounds like it, and if so, you deserve what you got and more." Of course, I was going to defend my friend.

"I lent her my darkness. Combined with the last energy I spotted in him, the last time we saw each other. Then sent my lines into her room, with his shape and copied memories. If she only wanted to talk to him, he would have been a perfect companion in conversation. I was not present, that is abhorrent," he grimaced like he had just eaten sour berries.

"Aha...."

"Think of it like a dog," he started another explanation. "You can see the dog, you can play with the dog, but you don't know what he's doing while he's in another room. So I gave her the dog, the one she wanted, the one she was crying after. It's not my fault that she turned it into a bunny and fucked the god out of it."

I laughed hysterically, so much that Rhylan got about ten decades older by the time I finished. "Stay there, I know just the cure." Fortunately, he obeyed and I removed my blanket and hurried into the kitchen to find everything we needed.

Chips, cereal, chocolate, mock cheese and bacon rashes, a full bottle of coke and a beer in case he wanted one. I had to carry everything on a huge breakfast tray and as soon as he saw me enter the bedroom; he jumped from the mattress to help me.

"Take off your clothes," I ordered while I did the same, keeping only my panties and socks.

Rhy's smile turned into a proud smirk and he made sure to remove his clothing slowly and in a very sexy way, showing how ready for me he was. We hadn't had sex in two days so I throbbed for him, fully recovered. Still, I wanted to prolong this for at least three more hours.

"Get under the blanket," I ordered and he did just that, looking a little surprised yet intrigued nonetheless.

As soon as he was settled and comfy, I placed the wide tray in the centre of the mattress and followed, cuddling myself in another blanket.

He looked at me with curious eyes, not knowing what to expect. Part of him could not help the excitement. Or at least I hoped so.

"What are we doing?" he finally asked when I grabbed the remote and made the TV screen pop from behind the wall cabinet it was hidden under.

"We're watching a movie," I replied with excitement.

He threw me a sly grin, surely remembering what happened the first time we watched a film. Now it was my time to raise a finger in the air and treat him like a puppy. "No," I said, my pointer finger straight in his face. "We are watching this, snacking on everything until our tummies hurt and once the credits roll, we cuddle in our blankies for a nap."

If Rhy could win an award for 'deepest frown in history' that would have been the perfect moment. I'm sure he didn't expect this, especially not after he'd told me he was falling in love with me and I refused to acknowledge his words.

"What are we watching?" he finally spoke in a grumpy tone, settling on the pillow and biting into a cucumber slice.

"It's my mom's favourite film. Well, used to be. I watch it about three or four times a year, whenever I miss her," I admitted and found the title on the list. That seemed to calm him down a bit.

"Titanic," he read the screen. "I don't think I've seen it," he admitted and my eyes gouged out, a dramatic gasp introducing my surprise.

"You haven't seen Titanic?" I had to make him repeat the answer just to make sure I heard him right.

"I don't engage in mundane activities unless it's business related, so I don't think so. What's it about?"

Oh sweet, innocent killer faerie. "It's a love story. You'll love it," I encouraged with a big smile. Planting a reassuring kiss on his lips, I pressed the play button.

Three hours and a half later, Rhylan accepted my cuddling offer after most of the snacks were finished. I curled onto his chest and laid my head on his biceps, while the faerie caressed my naked back in long, soothing strokes. The last thing I remember before falling asleep was his arm squeezing me tighter onto him.

Day 15

"I made peace with her... I think," a murmur came from my pillow.

"Good for you," I grumbled and turned to the other side, where sunlight beamed onto my face. What time was it?

"Sunshine, why is it that you are always sleeping?" Rhy shimmied to come closer to me and snatched me into his arms, spinning me towards the comfort of his touch.

"I had another event last night," I groaned and curled into him, basking in his warmth. Rhy's arms instantly wrapped around me, like they were finding home.

"Do you ever take time for yourself?" the faerie whispered as he planted a soft kiss on each of my eyelids, making me release a smile.

"There's nothing I wish more than to go away somewhere," I tilted my head and opened my eyes to meet him. The way he looked at me made my stomach tremble, like I was something precious, something worth a lot to him.

Rhy rested his head on the pillow to level with my own and blinked a smile as he asked, "Where would you like to go?"

I snorted at the million possibilities. Anywhere, really. Anywhere I could forget about the world and having to look the part all the time, some place where I didn't have to memorise lines and smile on demand.

"I don't know, Hawaii?" I giggled, imagining Rhylan, the mighty lord of darkness on a beach with those flower necklaces people wore there.

"Hawaii, huh? Are you planning on making every woman jealous of your perfect body casually resting on the beach?" he flicked my nose.

"Hardly perfect. And nope. I want to hide under one of those huge sunhats and drink my weight in alcohol, then have sex until I can't walk straight anymore," I admitted. I was fed up with showing my body. I wanted to party and let loose.

"Is that a challenge, sunshine?" His voice instantly darkened, roughened with desire. "If I take you to Hawaii, do you promise to scream my name instead of Jesus'?" His lips drew a wicked smile, a terrifying one.

"No, that's weird. I don't like saying the name of the guy I'm with. Plus, sometimes it would be like oh yes, guy I met in a bar at the after party, give it to me so good. Not sexy," I wrinkled my nose.

Rhy tensed by my side, the image of other men touching me visibly bothering him. Without saying another word, he rose from bed, not before gently placing my head back on the pillow and went through the hallways in search of something. I just stood there and waited, surprised and a bit frustrated with his attitude, yet I understood part of it was my fault.

Ever since he'd confessed his supposed love, I acted different around him. More weary and conservative, not letting my feelings roam free and my legs had remained shut. My body missed him, begged for him and every time he touched me I burnt for him, insides throbbing with desire and need. I wanted to give myself to him freely and unashamedly and let him do what he wished to my body.

But I could not. I could not let myself feel these things, even though my brain and my heart started to form an alliance against me and had gone team Rhylan. And if I acknowledged his words, I had to do the same with my own feelings, and could I really face that?

Deep down, I knew. I'd known even before our *mortal*

kombat sex edition. When he said those words, for a moment I thought everything would be perfect. That he loved me and I loved him and we could both find happiness together. The next second, I realised things like that didn't really happen. Especially not with an immortal faerie who wanted to kill everyone and who was also leaving in about three weeks to some underworld kingdom to hurt my sister's boyfriend.

"I have your purse, phone, charger and your birth control pills," Rhy returned to the bedroom like nothing happened.

"Okay…"

"Is there anything else you need?"

"I don't know," I responded with sarcasm. "A roof over my head, a shower, clothes, warmth, food, a cat maybe?"

There it was again, that wicked smile of his. Taking another step towards me, Rhy found those things and put them all in his pockets, then lunged over me in the bed and grabbed me in his arms, wrapping his legs around my own.

"Hold on tight," he whispered before darkness enveloped us.

Not knowing what would happen, I did as told and hugged the hell out of Rhy, pressing my body tightly to his. It felt like I was flying, movement flicking around us. At the same time, I was nestled into something warm, his waves of darkness enveloping me like a cloud, offering protection and stabilising my body. Whatever this was, I enjoyed it and I fully relaxed, basking in his warmth.

I soon came to realise that it was not only his body that released the heat, as a burst of sunlight made me abruptly close my eyes and allow them a moment to adjust. And I also felt warmth underneath me, so I shimmied my ass to discover I was splayed out on sand, Rhy casually resting on top of me, pinning my body under his. It took me a while to realise what had happened and to understand how I passed from being cuddled into my blanket to laying on a beach, all within the span of a minute. Had it even been that long?

Reading my expression, Rhy announced what I was too afraid to think. "Welcome to Hawaii," he smirked proudly, and helped me up.

We were on a beach, crystal clear water forming foamy waves around us.

In Hawaii.

He had brought me to Hawaii.

In my jammies.

"Are you crazy?" I started looking around, unsure if it was even legal for us to be here. Luckily, it was lunchtime, so most people were probably hiding from the sun and enjoying some food and drinks, because the area looked fairly deserted, so there weren't any witnesses to our strange appearance out of nowhere.

Except for the fact that I was still in my jammies, on a beach, with no documents or money, and I wasn't wearing sunscreen.

"You got my phone," I suddenly realised and turned to him, "and my purse," I added. He had planned this in the five minutes long conversation we had just then. "What if I said something silly, like wanting to visit the Arctic?" I pushed him, the palm of my hand having no effect over the hard muscles on his chest.

"I would have brought you a jacket first," he grinned, then found his phone and texted for a while.

"I can't be here, I have a charity gala tomorrow and an interview on Monday," I mentally started checking my to-do list, convinced that I was forgetting something, which made Rhy look at me for a second, then type some more into his phone.

"Who are you texting?" I pushed, taking a step towards him and coming closer to the screen. I fully expected Rhylan to protect it from my view, but he did no such thing, lowering his phone to allow me to see and read everything he was sending.

I immediately recognised the name. His good friend dirty-working Mark, the same man who arranged my surprise and filled my house with roses.

Rhylan: I'm in Hawaii, find me a honeymoon suite with a view and get them to bring as many yellow flowers as they can find. Champagne and strawberries. I need it in half an hour, also send a car to pick me from Makapu'u Beach.

Mark: Done boss, car will be there in 10. I'll change strawberries for dark chocolate, Ms Thompson's kindergarten records show an allergy to berries.

Rhylan: Fuck! Yeah, okay do that. Also get me sunscreen and makeup and a week's worth of ladies wardrobe in size six. Some clothes for me as well.

Mark: on it

"Does Mark do everything you tell him to?" I enquired, not unhooking my eyes from the screen.

"That's why I keep him alive," Rhy replied with his normal tone and fixed his gaze on me, probably to assess how I was taking our sudden vacation.

"What do you mean?" I started to worry about the safety of the guy, who obviously had nothing better to do apart from being on call for Rhylan 24/7. Not that I appreciated being spied on, especially not when the bastard found my address in a split second, though I was also grateful that he kept strawberries away from me. I hadn't touched them since I was five when I had a massive allergic reaction, and this was not a moment to experiment.

"He hacked one of my businesses," Rhy responded and started typing again to ask for a donation to be made in my name as an apology for my absence and for the interview to be rescheduled. "I hunted him down. Now he gets paid to do the things I need."

As soon as Mark replied to confirm, I felt a whiff of relief flowing over me. I could do this. Enjoy five days with Rhylan, just him and I and Hawaii. Might as well enjoy it.

By the time a black limo arrived to pick us up, I had started playing with the sand and taking scenery photos for my stories. Paradise indeed.

"Anwen is freaking out," I announced as Rhy passed me another drink. It became my favourite activity since we arrived and were greeted like absolute royalty. As soon as Rhylan uttered the name of the reservation we were under, Thompson, which I thought was a nice touch from Mark, the entire hotel staff had gone crazy with attentions.

Welcome drinks, personal staff if we needed anything at any point in our stay, complementary massages and dinners, spa treatments, mani-pedis, facials, premium services and everything one can ever want.

Staying true to his promise, Rhy kept bringing me drink after drink while I sat on a comfy lounge, watching the waves for hours on end. I didn't even need to move from our terrace, which had its own private part of the beach, only a hundred yards from our bed. I got to the point where I didn't exactly know if my eyes were drifting from the alcohol or if the sea had become more agitated before Rhy picked me up and carried me into the dining lounge, still open space and overlooking the beautiful waves, sitting me at a table and asking me to put something in my belly before I passed out from alcohol poisoning.

I remember eating chocolate eclairs, about three trays of them because who really cares if I get fat in Hawaii? After that, the evening became fuzzy. I do remember Rhylan's wandering tongue in between my legs and a couple of orgasms that put me straight to sleep.

One would think I would have learnt my lesson the next day, but no, here I was, drinking at ten in the morning with a faerie that was more than happy to babysit my ass. And posting photos of the guy.

As soon as I did it, I knew Anwen would see it, so I thought it would be easier to tag her and go with the flow.

"There isn't a moment in her life when that woman is not going crazy," Rhy chuckled and made himself comfier on the sand. Strange fact about fire faeries, they don't need sunblock. And they really enjoy anything that burns. Which gave me some ideas for later. He did nonetheless lather me in sunscreen from head to toe and placed an enormous hat on my head, just like I wanted.

"Hey, that is my sister you are talking about," I rasped and kicked his shoulder into the sand.

"And thank the god you are nothing alike," he grunted.

I wanted to protest, but the torchlights started calling to me and I immediately jumped from my seat and hurried towards the place where the hotel staff started setting up. I hated the idea of roasting a pig, although I had to see Rhylan with those flower garlands, so of course, we signed our attendance for the evening's luau party.

"Sunshine, I am all for your amusement, but come on," Rhy grimaced as I buttoned his shirt halfway through, leaving his stunning tattooed pecs out to be admired. As a payback for stealing me away, and also because I wanted to see him in something else, anything that wasn't black.

So I bought one of the traditional Hawaiian shirts with funky designs and forced the stunning faerie to wear it.

"It's orange and it has big red flowers on it. It looks like you're wearing flames," I tried to appease him, and I had to bite my lips to keep myself from having a laughing fit. Not that the shirt didn't look good on him, but because Rhy seemed as uncomfortable as a baby with a full nappy. He kept looking at me with shock, like he still couldn't believe I was making him do this.

"You are ruining my image…" he groaned, yet stepped to the door, accepting that the shirt would be a part of his party outfit.

"I'm sure you'll survive it," I replied and just as I said it, I quickly reached for my phone and snapped a few photos of him, just so I would never let him forget the moment.

As a punishment for my actions, Rhy smacked my ass on the hallway, making a stomping sound that echoed across the walls, and I knew one of my butt cheeks would stay red for at least an hour.

"I like to be spanked," I pushed my hair to the side and looked at him like it was nothing. Instead of bringing me triumph, the only thing the words succeeded to do was to raise challenge in his eyes. Big oopsie.

Rhy followed the torches and extended his arm for me to take, leading me towards the party like I was a queen. It only took us a few minutes to reach the stage they had built in the morning and we were welcomed with the flower garlands I had so desperately wanted to see around Rhy's neck. As soon as we reached the area, I took out my phone and announced another selfie time. He must have grown accustomed to my photos because he stopped and started posing as I took about twenty shots.

I kept my face in the position I already knew flattered me most, only shifting the angle just slightly, but Rhy adopted a full on photo mood and made a pose for each snap I took. Him laughing, grimacing, making a face, biting his lips seductively, kissing my cheek, resting his chin on my shoulder, staring at me like he was an ice sculpture, kissing me, biting his lips and my favourite, winking and showing a peace sign. That last one would definitely ruin his image.

We started greeting some people we had seen in the hotel, nodding and chatting casually about this or that, tasting every single cocktail, of course, and letting our hips follow the rhythm of the music. We swayed for a few songs, Rhy expertly spinning me around like we were on some kind of dancing show. In my defence, he was old. I don't even think guitars were invented when the faerie was born, so he had that benefit.

We kept away from the side of the actual luau. The last thing I wanted was to smell roasting animal parts, though I noticed Rhy's eyes darting to the food from time to time.

"Go, grab a bite," I pointed towards the area while we

were dancing, as an invitation.

"I'm okay…" he tried to convince himself yet just as he looked to see where I was pointing, his mouth must have watered because I spotted him swallowing quickly.

"Go eat something and I'll be here," I encouraged and he shook his head quickly to say no. I knew he wanted to, so I kept staring at him.

"Are you sure?" Rhy scanned my face, trying to read if this was a trick, but I wanted him to enjoy himself and just because I didn't eat meat, didn't mean that he had to starve through the night. Although I appreciated it.

"Go!" I pushed him slightly, urging him to move already, before all the good food was gone. "And bring another cocktail when you come back," I demanded and planted a kiss on his lips before I pushed him into the crowd and toward the food assortment tables.

I watched him slither through the crowd and admired his wide back from afar until I lost sight of him and decided to still enjoy the music on my own for another couple of minutes while I nursed what remained of my drink. One of the other guests showed up next to me and started mimicking my gestures, swaying to the sides just as I did, which made me chuckle.

He was a man in his thirties, dark-haired and fairly

handsome. I spotted him around the hotel a couple of times.

"I'm Adam, the night manager," he introduced himself and extended his hand to me, a silent dance invitation, which I accepted. The man came closer and got in a dance position, touching the middle of my back with one hand, while the other held mine, leaving an appropriate distance in between us.

"Nice to meet you. I'm Cressida," I nodded and continued dancing.

"Please allow me to keep you company while your partner returns. A woman so beautiful should not be left unaccompanied," he nodded to me and I smiled at the compliment. It didn't mean a thing. I was used to men popping out of nowhere and telling me the same thing over and over, while thinking no one else had even thought to speak to me in my life.

"He's grabbing a bite," I explained, and started humming the song.

"Are you not hungry?"

"I don't eat meat," I replied and the man offered to get me a tray of substitutes. I thanked him and explained I wasn't too hungry. And that is all I had time to say because the man paralysed in front of me, his arms and entire body tensing abruptly while his mouth expelled a wail, only audible to me. The next instant, a hand appeared on his neck and with a simple flick of the wrist, Adam's body turned with his back to me.

And facing Rhylan.

Rhylan, whose hand was cutting the man's air supply and strangling him in front of everyone.

"Rhylan!" I immediately moved and placed both my hands over his own, trying to release the man's neck from the faerie's hold, but the only thing I managed was to make him squeeze tighter. So tight that Adam was turning purple.

"Rhylan stop!" I shouted again, and some of the other guests must have realised what was happening because the music stopped abruptly and I heard voices everywhere around me.

"Rhylan!" I tried again and seeing how the man was dying and the faerie had absolutely no intention to let him go, I grabbed my empty glass from where I'd left it on a nearby table and threw it at Rhylan's head.

It was only then that he reacted and released the man, probably because of the surprise of taking a hit than my actual pleading screams. He looked at me in disbelief, eyes brimming with disappointment, and walked away through the crowd without saying a word.

I was so angry with him. I didn't understand what happened, why he reacted the way he did and when the surrounding people helped Adam stand and asked a million questions to check if he was okay, I knew it was my fault. I understood what he must have thought. Because I'd send him away and minutes later, he saw me with someone else. Just like that night he feared I would find someone new at the party. The night he confessed his feelings, which I blatantly chose to ignore, with no consideration.

"Rhylan!" I shouted his name and tried to find him in the crowd, but he was long gone, so I hurried back to the hotel, following the path of lit torches that led back to the entrance.

"Excuse me, have you seen a tall, dark-haired man? Very tall and handsome. He was wearing an orange shirt?" I asked a woman I found in the hallway and she waved her head no, though her eyes showed curiosity at my description.

I continued rallying through the hotel, asking everyone I could find, guests, staff, literally anyone, but he seemed to have vanished. Had he? I panicked at the thought. The last thing I wanted was to be left stranded in Hawaii without him. I wanted to scream, to shout, to punch things, although I had none of those options so, after about an hour of pointless searches, I headed to the beach and planned to swim until I had no breath left in me.

I returned to the room, holding a shred of hope that I might find him there, then headed out through the terrace and straight towards the beach, where I started walking through the darkness, following the moonshine into the waves and enjoying the way the water slapped my calves. About twenty minutes later, after I'd walked most of the private area of the beach, a sound brought back life into me.

"You'll catch a cold like that," I heard him from somewhere in the night and I started spinning, unable to see where his voice came from. Relief flooded my body. He hadn't disappeared. He hadn't abandoned me.

I followed the path where his voice sounded from to find him sitting on the wet sand, shirtless, watching the waves.

"You must have hated that shirt, huh?" I had to admit, he looked so much better without it, though I didn't think he would appreciate the compliment right in that moment.

"I only wore it because you liked it," he confessed and did not lose a beat to add, "I noticed how you like men who wear them." Of course, he was referring to the hotel manager.

"Rhylan, what is this about? Why are you like this? You could have killed the man," I scolded him, which made him huff.

"I can't do it, Cressida." His voice sounded hollow, defeated, his entire body echoing helplessness.

I immediately started shaking. "What do you mean?" He better not be saying what I thought he was about to, because then, my world would truly crumble.

"I'm done," he admitted and looked at me for a mere second before he turned to watch the waves again.

Oh my god, he was saying what I thought he was. I didn't think I could breathe, the meat on my bones started trembling and I fell on the sand by his side, but he did not seem to notice. Or if he did, the faerie did not care anymore. Not enough to help me up.

He started speaking again seconds later, while I was still struggling to calm down.

"I know I am the bad guy. I know that is what everyone says about me. The other faeries, Anwen, your internet. But even monsters can feel and get hurt."

I didn't know what to say, what to respond. I wanted to apologise, but really, what for? We were at a party and I received a dance invitation. And the man was a member of staff, trying to do his job and make the guests comfortable. Which I doubted he would ever do again. Had I really done something that bad?

"I thought things would change," Rhy continued speaking. "Ever since I met you, Cressida, I felt like a different male, I felt young again and untroubled. I hadn't laughed in centuries the way I did with you. And I thought…" he sighed, taking a moment to gather his thoughts. "I thought you would accept me for who I am, because I never told anyone so much about me as I did you. You made me remember things from old times, made me feel again and threw me on my ass when I deserved to. You are not afraid to show what you are thinking, and you are not afraid of me. Yet, I can't keep ignoring what I feel."

"Rhy…" I positioned myself better on the sand and planted my body closer to him.

"It matters to me, Cressida. I am terrified of the time we have left, I am obsessed with making every hour we have left count, with making you smile. Because every time you are happy, it brings air to my lungs. But above all else, above everything I want, I am a male. A male who wants you." He paused and exhaled a shuddering sigh, his next words a confession he did not make lightly. "Fuck Cressida, I want you so bad I would die for you over and over. And that's exactly what it feels like. When you ignore me. When you choose not to acknowledge my heart."

"Rhylan, that was the hotel manager, it's his job to take care of guests. I was alone and he just came to keep me company for a bit until you returned. It's not like I went and chose another man because I can't be on my own for five minutes and literally anyone is a suitable replacement. Stop thinking like that." It was my turn to reproach him, because I was sick of him thinking so little of himself. Who in their right mind would choose anyone else when they had Rhylan? I might as well close my legs forever because, after having this man, there would be no one else to top that. Or even to compare.

"Cressida, I love you," Rhy turned to me, moonlight shining in his eyes, making them look like glimmering stars. "I love you," he repeated with a whisper. "Yet, you are too scared of what this could mean to even acknowledge it," he sighed.

That was it. I was done. Done with all of this. He wanted me to show my feelings. Okay, fine, let's do it right now.

Without thinking, I launched myself onto him, throwing myself in his lap to straddle him. My movement was so quick that Rhy had to balance himself, and me along with him. I ambushed his lips with ire, devouring them, tongue swimming into his mouth and inundating it with my taste until I was sure I'd impregnated myself enough that he would miss it when I was gone.

My hands worked his zipper quickly and grabbed him, releasing his length from his pants and stroking it a couple of times to make it ready. Not that I had to put a lot of effort into it. The thing must have an alarm signal or something because every time my hand went there, it found it hard and ready.

Rhy continued to lean on his elbows, palms buried deep in the sand as I moved my panties to the side and aligned my core with him. With a gentle movement, I started lowering myself on him, careful to allow my body enough time to part for him and let him fill me, deep and slow, until I reached those two damned inches that didn't seem to fit inside of me no matter how hard I tried.

Rhy groaned and closed his eyes, enjoying the sensation of me around him, my slow exhales and my body still struggling to take all of him in. Only when I fully adjusted, I started to move, at first slowly, then more rapidly, eliciting moans from both our throats. At some point Rhy gave up, the desire to touch me overpowering his need to stay balanced and let himself fall on the sand, taking me along with him. Enjoying the newly found freedom of his hands, they reached for me, one settling on my breast and the other on my ass, following the rhythm I had become comfortable with.

I pushed myself into him, deeper and harder, determined to take all of him inside me, working him millimetre by millimetre until my wetness started dripping on him and allowing his cock to slide fully into me, touching the top of my core and raising sweet sensations I had never felt before.

"Oh god, Rhylan," I said as his tip pumped into me and into that part no one had ever touched before, making me go mad with sensation and pleasure.

"Yes…" he groaned. "Yes, Cressida."

He was the one to take full control now, my body too overwhelmed with everything he was doing to me, to my insides to have any sort of reaction.

"Fuck Rhy, yes," I screamed as he deepened his thrusts, ripping release from me.

"Say it again, say my name," he demanded while he shifted a hip and pulled my hair, keeping my spine straight and trapped, completely at his mercy.

"Rhylan…" I murmured, seeing red spots from the amount of pleasure my brain was experiencing.

"By the god," a sinful howl released from his throat as he too found pleasure and fell in the sand, taking me along with him, both panting like maniacs, air struggling to enter our lungs.

He looked at me with joy, with relief, with possession, and I knew. I knew then that no matter what happened in my life, no matter what he did, there would be no one else.

"I love you," I told him, letting go of my fears.

Day 17

After the wild few hours we shared at the beach, all the worry and troubles vanished from Rhylan's features. We took the time to relish in each moment and touch, taking turns to please one another with only the waves and moonlight witnessing our passion.

It was only when dawn started creeping in the sky, adding pink hues onto the clouds that we decided to return to the hotel and rest for a few hours, not before we both went for a quick swim to rid ourselves of all the sand and dried residue, then threw ourselves in between the sheets, Rhy cuddling me with care.

"Good morning, sunshine," I woke up with a kiss on my lips that lingered longer than necessary. I smiled and stretched under him, brimming like a cat who ate ten canaries.

"Morning babe," I whispered and gave him another quick

peck on the lips before turning to the side and nestling onto his chest.

"Babe, huh?" Rhy flicked my nose before tangling his fingers in my hair and scratching slightly. Head scratches were my kryptonite and he knew that. Lovely jerk.

"How would you like to be called, my liege?" I mocked. "Oh, mighty baby? Lord of the babes? Darky-larky boo?" I giggled.

"Darky-larky boo?" he frowned even though a quick grin appeared on his face.

"It stays!" I chuckled and pushed him back to jump over him on my way to the bathroom.

By the time I got out, teeth brushed, lips scrubbed, showered and body covered in sunscreen, a huge continental breakfast awaited on the bed, along with naked Rhy splayed onto his side.

"I asked Mark to send an apology cheque to the manager," Rhy pursed his lips as if he expected repercussion.

"That is a very nice gesture," I responded with a smile. I wasn't sure the guy would ever want to hear from Rhy again, though I kept the thought to myself, focusing my full attention on the faerie trapped under me.

"I don't remember ordering food, but I'll take it." I giggled and hurried to him instead, trapping him under my hips.

Even though the food looked delicious, I was once again hungry for him, only this time, I wanted to repay all the generosity he had shown so far and decided that I would be the one to worship his body that morning.

I started with kissing his lips, then moved to his neck and shoulder, biting lightly while my fingers started scratching his pecs. Rhy grinned, enjoying the sensation. By the time I started licking his abs, making my way dangerously south, he sensed what followed and for whatever reason, he grabbed my chin to stop me.

"Cress, no, you don't have to," he immediately said, and it was my turn to wrinkle my nose.

"But I want to," I insisted and made a gesture to push him back, yet Rhy did not bulge. "Oh, come on, I've been told I'm quite good at it," I kept insisting, unknowing if this last piece of information would stir curiosity or jealousy into my faerie lover.

"I can't," he insisted, which made me raise my head from his pelvis and find his gaze. "It's no point. I can't find pleasure that way," he admitted with a small grimace.

"What do you mean you can't find pleasure that way?"

I didn't understand his words or that slight annoyance he kept exposing while trying to retrieve his pelvis from under me, so I was determined to get to the bottom of this.

"Are you trying to tell me that you can't cum from a bj?" My eyes went wide with disbelief because there hasn't been a man in my life who hadn't enjoyed that. Generally, men were desperate for it.

He shook his head no, causing my frown to deepen. What in the hell? I had never found a man to not find his pleasure on the tongue of a partner, they were all desperate to receive the attention. Rhylan couldn't be that far off. And, stubborn as I was, I would not take no for an answer without even giving it a go.

"Do you mind if I try anyway?"

This was a challenge and mama needed to prove a point. Rhy rose his shoulders to say something like, *If you wanna waste your time go for it,* and leaned back on the bed. Then he reached for a couple of pillows and arranged them under his head.

"Can I at least enjoy the view?" he smirked wickedly.

"Sure, but that's not the only thing you're gonna enjoy," I promised him. Hopefully, I would keep that promise. More determined than ever in my life to tackle a blowjob, I pulled my hair up in a quick bun and stared at my opponent. Luckily, it was ready for me, so that part was sorted.

Trying to remember everything I knew about penises and

grateful for the anthology of porn scenes I had seen throughout my life, I started forming a strategy. Every man had to find pleasure that way, unless there was something wrong with his nerve endings or something. And seeing how he found his pleasure during sex, I doubted that was the case, so it must be a mental blockage. Not that I was an expert.

I thought about what I enjoyed when a man went down on me and what worked with the ones who did it well. Also, what worked when I did it myself. Sensation. Sensation and buildup.

Deciding to go for exactly that, I flicked the tip of my tongue over his erection and started to play with it, carefully watching his reactions to see what worked and what didn't. I started slowly, enjoying the taste of him with long movements, licking him unhurriedly and elegantly, since we had all the time in the world. I was weary at first, part of me wanting to give him the time of his life. The other part terrified that I would completely and utterly suck and be one more of the possible hundreds or thousands who thought they knew better.

I worked on it for about fifteen minutes with no chance of success, until Rhy exhaled an abrupt breath, just as I scraped my teeth along one of the thick veins of his cock.

"Does that feel good?" I quickly asked and he nodded,

watching me like a hawk. So of course, I did it again, a bit harder this time, eliciting a moan from the faerie.

I am a mother-fucking queen, I mentally padded myself on the shoulder. He was a teeth kind of guy. Which, for an immortal being who wanted to destroy the world and a fan of kinky rough sex, made absolute sense.

And if darky-larky boo enjoyed biting, I would, of course, indulge. Changing everything I knew about my performance, I started eating him rapidly, allowing my teeth to scrape the sides of him and my mouth working deeper, throat bobbing while my hands stroked the base of him, since it was impossible to take all that in my mouth.

Never mind, because he started purring like a hungry kitten, his hands tightening into fists, one of them grabbing the sheets and ripping into them with a sharp movement.

"Cressida…" Rhylan grunted, "fuck… that feels…"

He stopped, unable to find the words, unable to express what I assumed was a new sensation for him. So I continued, inhaling him into my mouth, scratching and scraping with my teeth until red marks appeared on the sides of his very erect member. He did not seem to mind, on the contrary. In an experimental attempt, I bit the tip of his cock to see what would happen and…

"Sunshine!" Rhylan screamed, a hand suddenly appearing

on the back of my head, grabbing the loose parts of my hair. I knew that movement, I recognised that need, so I dipped lower onto him, allowing him to push himself in my mouth and set a rhythm.

And there it was, mother of all glories, when only two minutes later, with a full on biting motion that went along his length, Rhy found his pleasure. The faerie escaped a rough scream, his eyes so wide I thought they would burst out of their sockets while with a few final thrusts, he freed his pleasure down my throat.

When he finally finished, I released him and, after quickly wiping my mouth with the back of my hand, threw him a knowing smile.

"What did you do?" he looked at me in disbelief, eyes still gauged out with pleasure.

"It's magic, babe," I giggled and within the next second I found myself splayed on the bed with Rhylan on top of me, with every intention of sliding in between my legs.

"Allow me to return the favour," was the only thing he said before his mouth lowered to my centre.

Day 19

"Are we ever going to leave this room?" Although I was more than comfortable laying on his chest and receiving back scratches, I had to get him out of the hotel, so before he had a chance to protest or to start the deliciously wicked activities that made us stay pinned to one another for the last couple of days, I came up with the idea. "Let's go shopping!"

Without giving him any time to protest, I rushed from bed, although the splendid waves we could see from the open space bedroom were calling me back to enjoy them from the comfort of his hug, and hurried to the bathroom.

Knowing he might make the apparition voodoo thing any minute, I ordered him to call his favourite hacker and get us a car in half an hour. To my surprise, he did just that and ten minutes later announced that the driver was already waiting at the reception.

I pitied the poor man who probably had to wait somewhere close, just in case Rhy and I might need him, but I decided to look fabulous so I took my sweet time, while devising the plan that had been gnawing at me since I confessed my love to Rhy.

Unwillingly, and especially before bed, while I nestled in his warmth and enjoyed the tenderness of the immortal faerie, I started daydreaming about our lives together.

Of course, I had absolutely no idea what would happen with his secret plans. When or if I would see him again after these days were over, but my brain fantasised on its own accord, making me imagine day-to-day life by his side. Simple things came to mind, like grocery runs, eating cake and watching movies, buying each other random presents and so on.

I wanted to offer him the full experience of a relationship, for him to be able to not just enjoy the passionate side of things, but the caring girlfriend I could be. Although we hadn't really discussed relationship status and I didn't know if that was a valid option, the fact that we both confessed to falling in love made it more real than any relationship I ever had.

When we arrived at the car, the driver had drinks prepared for us though we settled for cuddling each other in the back seat and kissing until our lips went numb. Rhy's hands lingered in some inadequate places, especially when someone else was there to witness my moans, yet the man did not seem to mind or even acknowledge our presence. Very professional indeed.

By the time we got to town, I had to rearrange my dress and my panties, while Rhy brushed his dishevelled hair with his fingers to make it look, once again, splendid. We thanked the driver and Rhy told him to wait for a call to pick us up again, while I nodded and blushed, silently thanking the man.

"What do you want to do?" the faerie asked after taking my hand and started to lead me towards a conglomerate of shops.

"I want to do some shopping on my own so I'll meet you back in…" I looked around to map my thoughts, "two hours?"

His face instantly dropped, obviously not expecting to be abandoned under any circumstance, but shopping by myself was pivotal for the surprise I was planning.

"Hey, I said I wanted to go shopping, I did not invite you to come along," I teased him and nudged him slowly with my shoulder.

"What am I supposed to do without you?" he continued to

look at me in disbelief, so I shrugged and pointed at a coffee shop.

"Get a coffee and deal with your plans to destroy the world?"

He rolled his eyes and nodded, then kissed me deeply, brushing the roof of my mouth with his tongue.

"An hour," he insisted, "any longer and I will cover the town in darkness until I get you back." It sounded sweet but very demonic. Luckily, it gave me another idea for a present so I quickly agreed.

"As you say, darky-larky boo," I grinned, knowing how he felt about his nickname.

I didn't have to look for Rhy, I only had to follow the stares of all the women in the shop to find him, because they were all diligently drooling into their drinks at the sight of him.

I planted an extra long kiss on his lips, just to make sure it delivered the message, then hugged him for even longer.

Yes sisters, he's mine.

"Ready to go?"

"I was ready fifty-nine minutes and fifty-nine seconds ago," Rhylan answered, still grumpy with my audacity to leave him on his own, though I hoped everything I planned would more than compensate for his wait.

Rhy left a bill on the table that paid for the cost of the coffee ten times over, then stood and rested his hand on my lower back, following closely after me.

"Where is the reap of your shopping spree?" he pointed to my small purse where I obviously couldn't hold many items.

"You'll see," I only responded and caught his hand, leading him to the cake shop where I had everything prepared.

I hoped that the owner I had just spoken to remembered the signal and that all my running around in the past hour would pay up.

"Let's get something to eat," I suggested just as we were passing the cake shop, trying to act like it had suddenly occurred to me.

"Here?" he frowned and pointed to a fancy restaurant on the other side of the street.

"Nah, I want something sweet," I wrinkled my nose and more or less pushed him through the door, where I hoped, I prayed, things would go according to plan. And...

"Happy birthday!!!" The owner, her staff and almost

everyone in the shop shouted as Rhy entered the establishment. I quickly hurried to the side to see his reaction. He was dumbfounded and staring at the people like they had just gone crazy.

"Just go with it, I'll explain as soon as we are seated," I whispered, hoping he would not get upset. I hadn't really thought things through and acted on impulse. In my defence, I had very little time to do everything.

Fortunately, Rhy nodded. I loved that about him, his ability to go with everything life threw at him and keep his elegance through it all. He smiled politely and thanked everyone, after which the owner lady led us to the table. A table where a gigantic birthday cake rested along with a booth full of presents.

"What is happening?" he murmured as he quietly followed the woman, who did not waste the opportunity to give him a big birthday hug and a kiss on the cheek.

"Okay, don't freak out, here's my line of thought," I felt the need to explain as soon as we were left alone. "You don't know when you were born, so you don't really know when it's your birthday. Which is a bit perfect because you can choose your own. So I kinda chose today for you, but you can change it, of course," I waved my hands immediately in defence of my idea because his eyes had started glinting in a strange way.

"When did you have time to plan this?" he barely spoke, throat bobbing.

"I didn't really, only had an hour, so some presents might not be as inspired," I bit my lips.

"Thank you, Cressida, this—" he paused, words stopping on his tongue and before I knew it, he jumped to my side of the booth and kissed me. Long and slow, taking the time to appreciate the contact of our lips and tongues.

I had to break it short because the anxiety was killing me and I wanted him to open the presents,

"Okay, first, the birthday wish," I urged, as I used the matches on the table to light the candles. I told the lady we had an inside joke, because I ordered four candles, making the number 1111. I lit each one and announced to Rhy, "Make a wish!"

I expected him to ignore or mock me, yet the faerie clearly enjoyed having his first ever birthday cake because he closed his eyes and after a long exhale, he took a deep breath in and blew all the candles in one go.

"I wished for…" he started to say, though I quickly placed my fingers over his mouth, sealing his lips.

"You can't say it. It has to be a secret for it to come true," I smiled as I announced the thing everyone seemed to know but him. Rhy nodded and pressed his finger into the icing, taking a generous bit and flicked it on my nose.

I started laughing while he giggled as well, then he made a point to lick away the cream from my face.

"Alright, alright, time for presents," I announced and grabbed one of the bags, placing it in front of him and watching how his eyes smiled with delight.

"Oh, no, you shouldn't have," he exclaimed, copying every adult who ever received a present, after which he hurriedly ripped the paper bag apart, to find a black t-shirt.

"Born to conquer the world," he read as he started chuckling. "You are amazing!" he laughed and kissed me over and over again.

For the next hour, Rhy spent the time opening present after present, enjoying cake and kisses, becoming more and more excited with each one. I worried for nothing, because even the silly ones, like a notebook that read *The Dark Lord* on a black cover made him laugh until tears filled his eyes, and I realised it was not about the value — although I did buy him a vintage Rolex — but the idea of the surprise. The fact that for once, he could find normalcy and eat a birthday cake, open a present and enjoy a kiss, just like any other man.

Day 20

"Till then, stay happy and wear that smile!" I waved to the camera and pressed the red circle button to stop the Instagram live which Rhy had insisted on being a part of. Of course, this meant that the life update I planned to chat about turned into a romance update because as soon as his head popped in — not only that, but my very sexy lover felt the need to appear shirtless on camera — the chat section started going crazy and I could barely answer around ten or maybe twenty out of the thousand questions cropping out on my feed.

I felt guilty for doing this. I wanted nothing more than to just be on holiday with Rhy, yet I also knew I could not ignore my job for so long and get away with it. Luckily, the photogenic and charismatic faerie charmed the public and gave me the perfect excuse to end the video quickly when he started to kiss my neck passionately.

"I like that," he bit my earlobe gently, "stay happy and wear that smile. You've said it before." It was the first time he spoke, during the video he had settled with making an appearance in the background and waving at the camera, then he took the seat next to mine and rested his head on my shoulder, gently kissing me or nibbling on my skin from time to time.

"It's my goodbye phrase, all vloggers have one," I explained and tilted my head to get a full grasp of his lips. I was ravenous for him and willing to let my body show it.

"Should I come up with a goodbye phrase of my own?" he grinned, basking in my need for him and blissfully lowering his fingers to in between my legs, his smirk deepening at the wetness he found there.

"As long as you come... and take me along with you," I giggled and spread my legs wider, displaying myself to him, to that hand that started the slow torture and the finger that flicked my bathing suit to the side.

"Sunshine…" he groaned as my hand lowered onto him, finding hardness.

"Let's skip to the good part," I moaned into his touch, pushing him onto the lounge-chair and hurrying to remove his pants as fast as I could. Without a second thought, I pulled what I wanted most and aligned my own body with his, pushing him into me within the next second.

"Cressida," Rhy rasped, hands reaching for me, to either impale me onto him or move me to the side, I did not know, did not care. I needed him and that urge felt primal, like nothing I'd felt before, making me forget the world, my manners and every desire apart from this. The contact of him and me, the sweet sensation his body was pouring into mine and the waves of pleasure that begged me to move further, deeper, more ferocious. Rhy groaned and grabbed my ass, moving me up and down, up and down with abrupt and desperate motions, his urge as heavy as my own.

I didn't care about the people who could see us or who could be walking on the beach and spot us fucking like maniacs. All I wanted was him. My soul belonged to him, the bond we were sharing every time our bodies conjoined driving me crazy to the point of obsession.

"Fuck, my love," he burst out just as I found my release and started squeezing him, taking him along with me as I went over the edge.

I only halted when his veins stopped pulsating and released him from inside of me, along with a trail of his desire, yet he did not move. Rhylan remained limp in my arms, panting and holding tight onto me like I was a life-saving jacket.

"I can't let you go," he announced, the answer to the question he probably read on my face. "Give me another minute," the faerie pleaded, and I did just that, relaxing into him while he remained pinned under me, still straddled by my anxious thighs.

"I don't wanna go back," I admitted, even though I was the reason we had to return because I had a morning event the next day. One that could not be cancelled, not when I worked for three years to get invited.

"I don't either, sunshine. I want to stay here forever and feast on you until you are physically unable to produce any more pleasure."

"Is that a promise, darky-larky boo?" I giggled, even though my stomach dropped at the prospect. Could anyone ever get tired of orgasms? I didn't think so.

Rhy huffed at the name, fully knowing he had no escape from it, yet his features turned sombre. I caressed his cheek and planted a kiss there, hoping to dissipate the clouds in his mind. It had the opposite effect.

"What is it? Did I do something wrong?"

His eyes shot to me, quickly waving. "Of course not, you are perfect," Rhy dropped a kiss on my forehead. And both my cheeks, to finally find my mouth and allow his tongue to roam free.

"I cannot be faithful to you while I'm gone," Rhy expelled the phrase as soon as the kiss ended, taking me from ecstasy to a very low drop of my stomach which caused bitter pain.

"Okay…" I replied, not sure if I thought the words or said them out loud.

"Sunshine, you are the elixir of my happiness," Rhy quickly cupped my face when I wanted to move from atop of him, locking me in place. "But I am duty bound."

"What, to fuck other people?" I frowned and pushed him, standing quickly and running inside, though after only a few steps, Rhy's hands tightened around me and turned me in the air. The faerie pressed his chest to mine and when I started struggling and pushing his shoulders, he threw me on the bed and pressed his weight over me, forcing me to face him, my body trapped under his own.

"Cressida, it's not something I want to do, but I need to be honest with you. You are the only person who accepted me as I am, and I want to reveal every part of me to you. Even the bad ones. Even the ones that would make you hate me. Because I love you. Like I never loved." The inky swirls in his eyes made my heart pound, however, my brain overtook the situation. This was not happening. I did not just let myself have all these feelings only to be abandoned after what, four days?

"People who love other people don't fuck other people, you dick!" I tried to wiggle and get myself free but those damned waves of darkness wrapped around my ankles and wrists, fully locking me in place, while Rhylan remained on top of me. I didn't even know if what I said made sense and I did not care. He got the gist of it.

"I am duty bound. Which is why I am trying to get myself free and this entire plan was set in motion," he tried to explain, which caused me to spit in his face.

"Fuck you!" I rasped and for a moment his expression turned savage, almost violent, like he wanted to retort, yet with a single blink he returned to his normal self.

"I love that filthy mouth of yours, and all the dirty things you do with it," the faerie said and pushed a kiss, shoving his tongue abruptly over mine, forcing my lips to part.

"Lemm... goooo!" I screamed from behind his tongue, even though the taste of him was already making my mind spin like crazy, urging emotions that were completely inadequate in this moment.

"Fuck, I love it when you are angry. Part of me wants to piss you off more and then fuck the wrath out of you," he panted from on top of me and there I was. Liquid again. I would never, ever again, blame a man for thinking with his dick.

"Let me go!" I shouted again, struggling to push that darkness away from me, and with it, Rhylan.

"No babe, you will listen, because you need to understand why I'm doing this." Within the next second, Rhylan pressed his hand over my mouth, covering every muffled insult I could get out and forcing my gaze to find his.

"Okay, we're doing this quick and dirty because I am crazy with desire for your sexy angry self right now and that promise to fuck the anger out remains. As soon as I'm done talking, you will be free, so the quicker you let me say my peace, the quicker your release," he said that last word with sinful delight, looking down to in between my legs then back to me.

Oh god, oh god, oh god, why was my brain malfunctioning so badly with this man? Of course I wanted to take him up on the offer, though I also wanted to be set free and kick him in the nuts, so I nodded once, signalling my understanding.

It was all Rhy needed before he started speaking, his body relaxing slightly over my own. "The Fire Kingdom has a king and a queen. Drahden and Shayeet. They have ruled for the past three centuries. She is more powerful than him, like I told you before, the king and all the court are mere puppets in her hands. And she is obsessed with beauty, although as you can imagine, after centuries her features are losing their shine. Which is why she draws energy and releases it to embellish herself," he finished those last words and removed his hold on my mouth, trialing my reaction.

I kept silent and blinked, urging him to continue and let me go already. "She needs to do this constantly and from various streams, I'm not sure if it has to do with the line of energy or her personal preference. The fact is that she uses the strongest males in the kingdom to reap it," his eyes pinned mine, urging me to understand the rest for myself, and no matter how much I tried, I did not get his meaning.

"Tell me," I tried to speak from under his fingers, needing to hear it. Because what my thoughts pushed was absolutely appalling.

"She fucks them. Us. There is a schedule which we all follow and via the means of our release, she then uses the bubbles of energy to embellish herself and become stronger," he admitted, features hardening. I shook my head abruptly, forcing his hand away.

"Rhy, you are telling me that this woman is raping people to be youthful?" My eyes went wide, unable to grasp the full extent of the information.

"It is not only for beauty, in time tissue, bones and muscles tend to get damaged." But basically yes, what he was telling me was that the freaking queen was fucking men to keep young.

"I have to present myself to her chambers every full moon, since my energy is the strongest. She is sated for about two weeks after that," Rhy added, raising shivers on my skin. He must have realised because he immediately let me go, his darkness fading from my extremities, body falling to the side.

"I am sorry, and I am trying to change that. And please believe that it is my duty and not my will that takes me there," he said, carefully pressing his lips to my cheek as a peace offering.

"I'm... I'm so sorry, Rhy," I shook my head, unable to think. Not knowing what to say. There was no jealousy left in me, only ire and hatred towards that beast of a woman. "Does it hurt?" My thoughts went to him and what he must feel when part of his essence was pulled away.

"It's nothing like I feel when I am with you. There is no pleasure," he quickly added, reassuring me while catching one of my hands in his. "It feels like...like I'm drained. Like a bad cold, I assume. I've never been sick like that, like humans get, though I've seen it happen. I can function, although not at full capacity and all I want to do is stay in a corner and wait it out.

It can take a few days to fully recover."

"Rhy... I..." What could I say? I am sorry you are being raped once a month? "Is there anything I can do?"

"I hope so, in the near future," he kissed my hand with gratitude. "But in the meantime, sunshine, let me enjoy you."

I didn't know what to say, what to do. He had clearly suffered through it for so long that no lingering sentiment of anger or self-pity remained. He spoke more fearful of how I would react rather that from pain regarding the situation he was in. I didn't know how he could do it, how he settled on the idea and accepted the abuse with regularity, still remaining able to enjoy his daily life.

Which made me understand his current situation even better, this desperation to do it all, to live it all at once, as if there was no tomorrow.

And I could only feel grateful to offer him that peace, along with the pleasure and love we were sharing. Even now, seconds after he'd confessed his pain to me, his tongue formed swirls on my pelvis, a silent request to let him enjoy the present.

I rested my head back and locked my fingers in his hair as Rhylan's head dipped in between my thighs before the world turned hazy and I started screaming in pleasure.

Day 21

Anwen's anger frightened me. I had never seen my friend in such a rage fit, and it was all directed at me. As soon as Rhy brought us back, I insisted on arriving at the Odstar home and seeing my sister, knowing I would not find her in the happiest mood. Although he protested, wanting to spend the night at my place, the faerie begrudgingly agreed and even went straight to his room to allow us the space to talk. What I did not expect was to find her exuding so much anger that I could barely get a word in.

She kept accusing Rhy of being evil personified, naming all the horrible things he was, what he had done throughout his long life. That is when I lost focus and sympathy, because even though I absolutely adored Anwen, she did not know him. Not like I did.

"But he is also kind when he wants to be, interesting, respectful and loyal, honest and so, so hot." I tried to downplay it with the last part, not that I was not correct in every aspect.

"Because he had hundreds of years to practice it!" Anwen started again, her indignation splintering into a hundred directions, each one pointing at a negative aspect of my lover.

"Anwen, there are things you don't know yet, things he needs to tell you. He has his reasons," I tried to calm her down, even though I could not tell her a thing. It was not my place nor could I decide how much of Rhy's life she had to know. This was a very much needed conversation that both of them had to settle. And soon.

"Stop defending him!" she started shouting again and my heart began racing, fearing that Rhy would come in at any second and get involved. The last thing anyone needed was for their relationship to worsen after this, because god knows it was barely hanging by a thread.

After consistently insisting and asking me a hundred times why I kept defending Rhylan, I decided to tell her the truth, hoping that if she saw the good side of him and how worthy of love the man was, she might give him another chance. I allowed the words to drift from my mouth, hoping to find understanding.

"I love him," I confessed slowly, barely pronouncing the words, terrified of the effect they might have on her.

And I was right. If there was one defining thing about the Odstars, that would be stubbornness. Funny thing, I believe they all got that from Rhylan. So what happens when a stubborn woman trying to defend her sister and the maker of that very same feeling get together? A door gets ripped into pieces and a faerie almost kills my friend.

"Rhy…" I announced my panic at the sight of the two of them when I followed Anwen to his room, to find the door hinges ripped from the wooden frame and Rhylan pinning Anwen in bed, his darkness rippling threateningly around her.

Fortunately, at least one of them could exercise control, because as soon as he turned to me, Rhy's expression softened and released my friend, appearing by my side in the next second.

The sight of us together, the way Rhy leaned protectively over me, my hand cupped in his, must have raised demons in Anwen because she shouted from the top of her lungs, acting like a wounded beast. "This ends now!" Then she blinked and added, "You will not see Cressi again, or I will break the contract and remove you from this house."

I shook my head in silent disapproval. If she would only listen. "Anwen, there are things you don't understand," I decided to be the one who spoke first, knowing that Rhy didn't care as much about her feelings and might mess things up, so I stepped in front of him, trying to dissipate her anger and focus her attention towards me.

"You cannot break the contract, you already signed it." Of course the freaking faerie had to say something to piss her off just then, right at the moment when I was trying to appease her.

What happened next was out of my control, and I assumed that the entire household witnessed the encounter, especially since it was past midnight and the two of them raged at one another like two stray cats fighting for territory.

By the time I tried to close the door or at least jiggle it back into the doorframe as much as I could, Anwen demanded Rhy to do the appearing thing and take her to the forest. My heart started pulsating with terror, could he even do that after he'd transported me halfway across the world from Hawaii? I remembered what he confessed about the queen, how losing parts of his energy made him feel sick.

Probably reading the panic in my gaze, Rhy offered to take her the following day, but Anwen kept insisting to go right that second. With a sad look on his face and without unhooking his eyes from mine, a silent apology protruding through his eyelashes, Rhy grabbed my sister and disappeared, leaving me alone in the room.

I waited there for about an hour, full of worry for both of them. Anwen would get her answers, so at least that was a good thing. Still, Rhy had to go into enemy territory where everyone wanted a piece of him.

And here I was, a woman with no power who loved them both.

After realising they weren't coming back, I ubered home and wrapped myself in the blankets that still carried Rhy's scent, forcing my heart to settle.

Ironically enough, I had one of the best days of my career. The interview went amazing and the company offered me an extended contract, one that paid three times more than my asking price, with international features for the following four years. I was then invited to dinner with the directors and marketing team to a fancy restaurant where we finalised the details and celebrated the collaboration, which would be spread all over the media during the next couple of days.

I tried to keep all my focus on them and avert my attention

from the phone that had not displayed Rhy's name on the damned screen once. After a few bottles of champagne, many fabulous photos and lots of handshakes, I finally managed to escape the long dinner and headed back home, where I hoped he would be waiting.

Nope. Sulking in my solitude, I ran a long bath and soaked for an hour, phone thrown on the nightstand, away from my sight. I tried to distract myself with a rom-com on Netflix, finally using the TV that came installed in the bathroom, which always made me feel weird. I didn't really understand the need to have a TV there and why the previous owner had it installed until this very second, when my boobs were perfectly covered by bubbles and my head rested comfortably on the side, having a perfect angle to watch the screen.

Halfway through the movie, with my muscles extra relaxed from the mix of hot water and alcohol, I wrapped myself in a comfy bathrobe and went to bed, spreading my wet hair on the pillow.

A warm embrace made me react and open my eyes, blinking to find darkness across the room and Rhy's breath on my neck, cuddling close to me.

"I was worried about you," I confessed, half-asleep.

He answered with a few kisses on the shell of my ear. "And that is why I love you so much. Because even knowing

I cannot die, you still worry about me." Even though the words were sweet, his breath felt uneven, worried, so I immediately turned to him to find his eyes glinting in the darkness.

"What happened? Is Anwen okay? Is everything—"

"Shhh, she's okay, everyone is okay," he stopped my words and turned me back to my initial position, planting his bare chest on my back and cuddling tighter.

"We'll talk more tomorrow. Let's just sleep for a few hours," he voiced slowly, making me realise how tired he was.

"Okay…" I whispered back and shimmied out of my robe, allowing my naked skin to find his while muscular arms covered my body, pulling me tighter into his embrace.

Day 22

"What do you mean, you have to go? You were supposed to stay for three more weeks." I did not want to burst the way I did, not after he'd been so patient and explained everything that happened in the forest, giving me all the details of the faeries and the guy who replaced Ansgar. But this information was intolerable. Rhy and I were just beginning our journey and I needed more days with him, more time. I wasn't ready to let him go, not now that I'd found him.

"I know…" he muttered from where he was sitting on the bed, eyes facing the floor rather than my features.

"So what happened? Why this sudden change?" I questioned, holding back the urge to push him, to do something to show my anger.

"Things happened, sunshine. Things out of my control.

They messed it up... everything." Rhy shook his head from thoughts flashing in front of his eyes. "These couple of days that we get are more than I can afford, but by the god, I will not leave you yet." As he said the words, he stood abruptly and approached me, moving to grab me in his arms. I stepped away.

This was not me, this was not my life. I wasn't someone who he could decide when to leave. I wasn't... "No. If you leave, you leave now. I will not pretend to be happy for your benefit while my heart is breaking. What do you want me to do? Act like a happy girlfriend until you call me one day and tell me I will never see you again?"

"Cressida, I am not planning to leave your side. You may love me or hate me, but I am staying," he took the final step and forced his arms around me, pressing me to his chest in a hug I did not want, yet one that my body gladly accepted. My first instinct was to fight, to push him away and make him suffer, to reject his closeness so he could see my pain. However, as soon as I touched him, I realised his muscles were trembling. Slowly, barely noticeable, but enough for me to realise that he too had been suffering, his entire being craving this embrace.

I let myself go, wrapping my arms around his neck and reaching for the back of his head to present gentle scratches as a peace offering. As soon as my fingernails threaded through his hair, he relaxed into me, bringing his head closer to the palm of my hand like a cat who begged for attention.

We stayed like that, enjoying one another, touching and caressing parts of our bodies and never once letting go completely of that embrace. Our fingertips had the mission to remember the other's body, their curves and muscles, the feel of their hair and smooth skin.

Rhy was the first to break the connection, knees bending to let his body drop in front of me in an abrupt motion. His eyes moved slowly, taking me in inch by inch, starting from my toes until he reached my face. And my surprised expression.

Then he looked at me, those adamant eyes piercing through me like never before, when two words escaped his mouth. Two words that would change the rest of my life. "Marry me."

I froze. "I'm sorry, what?" I bent towards him to make sure I'd heard him right, but that all-knowing grin told me everything I needed to know.

"Of course you are going to make me say it again," Rhy sighed slowly, keeping his position on his knees, firmly planted on the floor, eyes on me. "Cressida Thompson, love of my very, very long life, will you do me the honour of becoming my wife?"

Did he just say love of his life or was I imagining things? He must have, because I swear that is what I heard, but how could that even be possible? He must have been with thousands of women throughout his life, and somehow he wanted me? Thousands of women... I let that sink in for a bit, numbers rolling in front of my eyes. Images of populating a village with all his lovers came to mind. Lovers? Had he been with men too? Men and women? At the same time? Now my mind started rolling on faerie orgies.

"Do I have to make a grand gesture?" Rhylan smirked, and I looked back at him to find him still on his knees and he was... blushing. Was I making Rhy uncomfortable?

"Are you sure?" I bent so low that I was practically sitting on top of him while he remained kneeling like I was some kind of queen.

"I was never more sure of anything in my entire life," he exclaimed in the next second, reassuring me of his decision. And I had to give it to him, the determination in his voice sounded very convincing.

"Have you been married before? Is this a harem kind of situation where you have a wife in every country or something?" It sounded silly, but I had to check. It's better to ask and look stupid than to find unpleasant surprises.

Probably sick of the whole situation, Rhy dropped to the floor and took me with him, making me straddle him.

He cupped my face with both his hands, squeezing me tightly. The faerie's eyes dripped ink into mine as he blinked a few times, probably trying to decipher what was going on in my mind.

"Why is it that I can't read you?" he murmured and I had no clue what he was talking about. Also, it wasn't as important as the proposal I had just messed up.

"What are you feeling right now? Right this second?" His gaze darted to my hair, following the waves created overnight by the silk pillow. He took a few seconds to scan it, looking somewhere around my head. Was my hair frizzy today or something?

"I'm…" I took a moment to clear my mind and focus on my feelings while Rhy continued to scan the air around my head. What was happening with my hair today? "I'm excited. Happy. Scared and worried at the same time," I confessed.

"Four feelings. And I can't see any of them," Rhy talked to himself out loud. I had no idea what he meant… Fine, if he wanted to see them, then I'll show them to him.

I pressed my lips on his, kissing him excitedly at first, my tongue finding his own and sucking the taste, then reached the roof of his mouth, making sure that he felt me and my taste.

"Happy now?" I asked when my lips unhooked from his, pleased with myself.

"Do I have your permission to take that as a yes?" he grinned proudly, and I smiled, defeated.

"Yes, Rhylan, I want to marry you," I curved my lips wider, displaying a deep smile. "But I am *not* taking your name, that needs to be made clear straight away. My surname is all that's left from my parents, so not planning to change that." Before he had a chance to reply, I wanted to check how it felt in my mouth so I said it out loud, joining the sounds together for the very first time. "Cressida Gordon." I immediately grimaced. It felt wrong, it sounded wrong. Nope, not doing it.

"Fine with me." I expected him to protest more, yet there he was, letting me set all the rules on this marriage thing.

"And when are we supposed to get married? Your horrid news gives us like... another full day together?" I questioned. He must have thought it silly, because his eyebrows shot up.

"Now, of course," he said it like it was the most obvious thing in the world and with a smirk, he added. "Go get dressed girl, we're getting married."

"Now? As in now, now?" I shot up, realising I was in the bathrobe from yesterday and had terrible hair.

"You can take your time to get ready, of course," Rhy

noted and stood as well, only to then throw himself on the bed and make himself comfortable with three of my pillows.

"Married in Vegas!" I threw a fist up in the air, copying the action of a superhero while also expressing an idea. And since I was already making a fool of myself, I continued. "With no notice." I changed my stance into a fighting one. "Will they make it?" I finished dorkily while hitting the air.

"They will make it, I can assure you." Rhy already reached for his phone, probably to text his favourite hacker to get things sorted for us, but I snatched it from his hand.

"No, no, no. If we're doing this, we're doing it like normal people," I demanded. Seeing the surprise on his face, I added my request. "I want to get married by Elvis, in one of those churches you can pop in and queue with drunk couples. And pay the premium package so they can record us, just like in the movies," I explained with excitement, guarding his phone with my life. "That's my condition."

"We will do it just like you want to, sunshine," Rhy agreed with one of his dashing smiles and in all fairness, I didn't think he gave a damn where we got married, as long as we did it. "May I please have my phone back to at least organise our wedding night and treat you like the goddess you are?"

"Well... if you put it like that..." I threw him back the phone and rushed into the bathroom to get ready. I had no idea how he did it, because Rhy needed a maximum of two minutes of preparation to look fresh and absolutely stunning while I needed half an hour for make-up and another hour for hair, but this was not a time to concern myself with faerie business. It was a time to make myself look pretty.

I arranged my hair and applied make-up, which took around two hours until I was satisfied with the results and another hour to change into ten outfits. I finally decided on a black opera dress, knowing it would match Rhy's favorite choice of designer suit and black shirt he always loved to wear. When I was finally ready, I announced it through the door and took a moment to think about my parents.

Then I stepped out in all my glory, making my fiancee-of-one-afternoon's' mouth drop to the floor. Were he not immortal, I would have been worried about him, because I swear Rhylan stopped breathing.

"You look—" he stumbled on the words. "Beautiful." He didn't seem too happy with that, so he added. "Stunning." Then another compliment arrived. "Gorgeous."

"And ready to get married," I added with a proud smile.

I vaguely remember what happened next. Rhy grabbed me in his arms and squeezed me tightly onto him, then we were in Vegas, at the busy entrance of a hotel. Rhy went to the reception desk and announced our arrival, and just like in

Hawaii, as soon as they heard the name Thompson they started buzzing, to which my husband-to-be told them we would return in an hour and prefer to be undisturbed for the rest of our stay.

A black limo appeared outside by the time we were done and Rhy, always the gentleman, opened the door to invite me inside. As soon as I stepped in, my nostrils were inundated by the smell of roses and when my eyes adjusted to the darkness, where only a few dim lights flickered, I saw that the majority of the space was occupied by hundreds of yellow roses, the same ones Rhy had surprised me with at the beginning, along with a bottle of champagne and two glasses. When he joined me in the car I did not hesitate to kiss him, a silent thank you. For everything he was doing. For all the times he took care of me like no other man had done before. For all the thoughtful sweet gestures he didn't have to do, but did anyway.

"We also have champagne if my lady needs some courage," he pointed to where the bottle rested in a bucket of ice.

"Later, make me your wife first." I took the next minute to feast on his lips before he had another chance to speak.

"It is the other way round, you are making me your husband. Offering me the highest honour," Rhylan gently bent at the waist in an attempt of a bow and placed a kiss on my knuckles.

I wanted a church of Elvis experience and that is exactly what I got. Even though part of me fully expected Rhy to interfere somehow, he stayed quiet and only did the necessary on our arrival. There was no big parade, no extra roses or grand gestures.

We arrived at the reception and a grumpy lady looked at us with a big old frown, judging our outfits. It was not a guess, we knew exactly what she was thinking because the first words out of her mouth were, "If you are this rich, why the hell don't you go to one of the casino churches? They give free champagne there."

I didn't know how to react. Luckily Rhy answered. "We do not require any champagne, thank you though."

The woman looked at him like he was three shades of crazy, then sighed and asked to see some documents. We both presented our passports and when the receptionist spotted Rhylan's, she had another idea, a deep condescending frown appearing on her already wrinkled forehead.

"Ha, is this some kind of citizenship scam?" This time she

looked at us like we were delinquents, her eyes turning into judging slits, burning into us. I had no idea where this was coming from, how this was even possible. Here we were, trying to get married, and this woman looked to be on the verge of phoning the police.

"No..." I responded, not knowing what else to say.

"Tell that to Homeland Security." Then she started muttering about another form and turned her back to us to find a document from a very old archive of folders. Rhylan and I looked at each other with curiosity and horror, neither of us knowing what to say or do in this situation.

Finally, when she found a yellowy paper, she made us both sign it, mentioning that at least this way, she was covered.

I didn't know if I wanted to laugh or cry. Rhy did most of the talking and kept his composure up until we reached the payment part.

"That'll be two hundred. If you want to say your own vows, it's three hundred. And seeing how you are rich and all, you could also leave a good tip."

I didn't even think about bringing cash. I was used to paying card all my life; fortunately, Rhy saved the day and placed five one hundred bills on the counter.

"Vows or no vows?" she asked, the fact that she received

a huge tip not counting towards her attitude.

"We'll say our vows privately, thank you," Rhy responded and touched my hand reassuringly.

"Very well, Elvis is waiting," the woman said as she quickly grabbed three bills and shoved them in her pocket.

The experience with the priest wasn't at all more enjoyable, if he could even be called that. A man in an Elvis costume and wig was on his phone when we entered the room, only three other chairs available. Instead of showing a smile or a small display of content for a couple about to marry, or even the fact that he had customers, he made sure to let us know that we were bothering him and he'd rather be on his phone.

The ceremony lasted five minutes give or take and I didn't remember most of it. We said the words, we kissed, signed the documents, and received the certificate in an envelope, then we were out. They didn't even let us exchange rings. Not that we had prepared anything, anyway…

"Is that really what you had in mind?" Rhy looked at me in disbelief as we left the building, goose flesh crawling on his skin from the dreadful experience.

"I really don't know," I admitted. I was shocked by how everything went down and I did not feel married or that anything had changed between us at all. How does one even feel married? "They make it so much cooler in the movies," I tried to defend myself, still shook with the rushed and not-at-all-like-I-dreamt-it experience.

"That's because people are generally drunk," Rhy tried to comfort me as we walked back to the car.

"Yeah... we should have gotten drunk," I admitted, regretting my choice from before.

"Wife," Rhy said with a smile as he opened the car door for me.

"Thank you, husband," I smiled back.

Day 23

My husband's hands were all over me during the car ride and I did not complain once, enjoying the ecstatic smile he was displaying. I don't think I ever saw him so happy, accomplished and relaxed, all at the same time. He had this glow about him, like all the troubles in the world had suddenly disappeared, and it was contagious.

Rhy manifested his joy by telling the driver about ten times that I was his wife, splashing champagne all over the car and spraying both of us with it, then kissing me with maddening passion, while his hands reacquainted themselves with parts of my body.

When we reached the hotel, he continued to announce our marriage to everyone in sight while he carried me in his arms like a princess. Honestly, I didn't mind and I loved being nestled in his strong arms, so I giggled every time he started pestering someone about our marriage, laughing out loud when people threw him careful looks, like he was three shades of crazy.

The elevator journey was a blast, with Rhy pressing me against the wall and lifting my dress up just enough to find the inside of my thighs. And since we booked the honeymoon suite, which was the penthouse, he had a good minute or two to tease me to the point where my legs started shaking.

As soon as the doors opened, my husband grabbed me into his arms yet again and crossed the threshold, which in this case turned out to be the elevator doors into a huge entryway full of lit candles where a trail of rose petals formed a pathway towards the bedroom.

I tilted my head to Rhy, to find his eyes burning, a perfect synchrony with the candlelight. "Of course you had to go all out," I pointed, and he immediately retorted.

"After that wedding experience, forgive me for wanting to regain a sense of normalcy."

Poor man was really traumatised and honestly, I could not blame him, because those ten minutes or so had been the weirdest of my entire life.

"I don't even feel married," I admitted. I don't know what I expected, for some kind of rainbow to appear over me?

Challenge rose on my lover's face and with that wicked smile that both terrified and delighted me, he murmured into the shell of my ear. "Allow me to rectify that, wife."

Darkness enveloped the room, so deep that I could barely spot the faint sparkles of the candles, but they looked so far away they might as well have been in a different universe. Rhylan remained corporeal by my side, yet shadows and ripples of darkness steamed from his body and poured in every corner of the room, inundating the space with inky blackness.

I felt his hands around my body and his lips on my neck, while the zipper of my dress magically became undone, even though one of his hands rested on my breasts and the other dangerously close to my pelvis.

Clothing slipped from me in the next instant, leaving my body fully exposed to him, to his darkness and power. Somehow, we reached the bed. To be more accurate, *I* reached the bed, those lines of darkness, as he called them, transporting me atop the silk covers.

I didn't exactly know where Rhylan was, even though I heard his rugged breathing, the night around felt so heavy that I could not sense anything around me. It felt like I was blindfolded.

I patted the covers around, trying to find him, to reach for him, though a shrivel of darkness wrapped around my wrist like a rope and pulled my hand away, keeping it trapped above my head. The instant I gasped, my left arm followed, leaving me completely bare and defenceless.

"Rhy…" I murmured, anticipation lingering in my voice.

"No, I am your husband," he responded from the darkness, a voice so wicked it made me throb in all the right places. I did not know what he was about to do, only that I would remember it for the rest of my life.

With it, Rhy's tongue made its way in between my legs, along with his head and strong arms that were splaying me open for him. I still could not see him, but I felt his fingers digging into the inside of my thighs and his locks of hair moving uncontrollably, leaving behind a tickling sensation as his mouth worked me to the point of exhaustion.

He did not take it slow, did not linger or bask in the taste of me as he had done before, instead he ate at me like he had to gulp me down to make sure no one else could steal me away. Rhylan was ravenous and merciless, eliciting moan after moan from my lips, playing with my clit with that sinful mouth while two fingers pumped into me, pleasuring me from the inside, making sure to follow the same rhythm as his tongue.

"Rhy…" I could barely breathe. I wanted him to stop, the sensation was too much, and I had already found release, but he kept stroking me to the point of sweet pain, to where I did not know what was happening to my body. In a weak attempt to defend what remained of my insides, I pressed my legs together, trying to remove his tongue and his head from the centre of me, to offer myself at least a few seconds of pause, just enough to regain control of my senses.

That was a big mistake, because the same darkness that restricted my hands did the same with my legs, splaying them wide enough for Rhylan to fit just fine and even have wiggle room, while my poor self was tied up and completely powerless to his plans.

With a satisfied grin I could sense more than see, Rhy bowed his head back in between my legs and resumed his feast, this time adding a third finger, forcing my body to split wider for him, some sort of punishment for having dared to interrupt his honeymoon dinner.

My husband's tongue continued its bursting torture, and all I had left to fight were my hips, which he rested over, and I did not have enough strength left to try to wiggle him away.

"Rhylan," I shouted his name as those damned fingers pierced abruptly into me, cupping me from the inside in such torturous ways.

I got what I wanted, I made him stop, even just for a second.

"Does it hurt?" his voice sounded gruff, fingers and tongue instantly halting.

"No, but..." Before I could continue, the faerie resumed his work, mouth only stopping to say, "In that case, be a good wifey and listen to your husband." And with that, he fully returned to his activities. It was so dark that I had absolutely no clue how he looked and I didn't think he could breathe from down there, his mouth drenched in me and my taste, his entire face fully nestled in between my legs.

I was all sensation, my touch and view restricted, allowed to only feel him. To only think of him. To stop existing beyond that point where he worked me so expertly and so, so wickedly.

I found release for a second time, rasping my orgasm so loud that it sounded like someone was ripping me in half. Which.... to be honest...

Satisfied with his work, Rhy removed the darkness from around us, allowing me to admire his taut muscles and realise that he too, had undressed. His entire face was wet, wet with my release and seeing him like that made me want him more than ever.

I wanted to move to him, to grab him, to throw myself on top of him and tease him like he did with me, yet my restrictions remained.

I wiggled my wrists above my head, a silent request for him to release them, but my naiveté gained a smirk and before I knew it, I was being turned, more ripples of darkness enveloping me to help the motion while Rhylan did not shift his position. I had to twist my neck to be able to continue looking at him as my body was being placed to lay on my front, leaving my back exposed to his mercy.

I had one guess as to what his plan followed, and of course I guessed correctly, because his mouth resumed its licking and panting, only this time it went upwards. His hands splayed my ass, making enough room for his mouth to reach and oh my goodness, the way his tongue moved was a demonic thing. I rolled my hips, trying to get him away, a mixture of pleasure and shame ripping at me.

It became an unspoken rule. Every time I wanted to remove a part of my body from his hold, it was restricted by those ripples of darkness, keeping me in hold and pinned to their master's will. He ate at me to the point of ecstasy, my asscheeks slapping his face from the hastiness of his motions and as soon as those two fingers found its way into my pussy, I was done. Third time champion for the evening, newlywed Cressida, thank you very much.

I panted, even my lungs exhausted with the heaviness of my pleasure, yet as soon as I dared think I would be released, those two fingers continued to move inside of me. A whip of his shadows formed around my thighs, lifting me just enough in the air to be perfectly positioned for him, and I soon realised why Rhy needed external help to get a hold of me, as he started working me from three different angles. His fingers caressed my clit, torturing me in the way they were already very acquainted with. This time, he started working my ass as well, another finger opening me for him.

Can I die from sex? Is that physically possible? Because that's what I wanted. I was so filled by him that I lost control of everything. I forgot my name, what I wanted and who I was. The only thing that mattered in the world were those three points of pleasure and the sensation I had never experienced before.

I turned to Rhylan, trying to express with my eyes what my words had long forgotten. I wanted to scream, to shout, to show everything that enveloped my body, but he only glanced at me and blinked, pleased with the torture he was inflicting.

"I know…" he whispered, voicing everything I couldn't, the acknowledgement of the pleasure he was drilling into me, rising a proud smirk on his face.

And I didn't know pleasure can be anything more than what was happening to me right then, until he asked, "Where do you want me?" fingers abruptly tightening inside of me for emphasis.

How could I even choose? I wanted him. I did not care how, or when, or where.

"Everywhere," I replied earnestly, completely and fully throwing myself at his mercy.

A pleased groan escaped his throat as he slammed into me within the next second. Surprisingly, he slid in quite gently and I must have been so ready for him that his thickness was eased by all the orgasms I had before.

"Fuck, wife, you feel so good," he grunted as he slammed harder into me, pushing deeper into my insides, up until the point where my stomach twitched from pressure.

I could not get used to the rhythm, he was hard and ruthless to only change into deep and slow, not allowing me an instant of peace and just when I thought I was about to find release again, he retrieved from me to take me from further behind, splaying my other side wide open to receive him while his hand continued to work my clit.

He kept amusing himself like that, changing directions and positions, taking me from one side, then changing to the other, having me splay wide for him every time, all the while keeping me restrained.

All I could do was scream, pant, moan, cuss and expel release after release, until the bed was soaked with the evidence of my pleasure.

I probably said "Fuck, Rhylan" so many times that the walls might recognise it as the new alarm trigger while my husband introduced me to every single pleasurable sensation known to the human body until we both felt trapped into his darkness, losing track of time.

Day 24

"Good morning," I whispered as soon as Rhy's adamant eyes opened to find mine. After the exquisite torture I had endured for hours, as soon as he let himself find release, something cracked inside my faerie. He stopped, looking at me with a weird mix of passion and heartbreak, finally allowing the darkness that held me into position to vanish.

As soon as my body was free, hands finally enjoying liberation, I sprang to him, wrapping him in my arms.

Rhy allowed himself to drop into my embrace and fully fall into me, taking abrupt gasps at the contact of our skin. Innately, his hands wrapped around my waist and crushed me to him, head resting on my chest while the rest of his body remained limp, letting his full weight splay onto the bed and on top of me.

"It's okay," I murmured and caressed his hair, planting soft kisses on his forehead while his fingers still gripped me tight, holding me like he was about to fall into an abyss and I was the only thing keeping him alive.

"It's okay," I echoed, trailing a hand down his shoulder and as much as I could reach from his back, while the other one held him tightly. "It's alright," I said it again, even though we both realised the falsity of the words.

He shuddered, utterly and completely broken in my arms, letting go of the last shred of control, the one he had tried to prolong during the many hours he had pleased me, not wanting to stop because that is all we had left. All that kept us together, and we both knew that as soon as it finished, we'd be forced to face reality.

A reality where we had to be apart, not knowing when or how we would see each other again.

"I don't want to go, I don't want to leave you," Rhy whispered from inside the embrace, words so broken that they forced my heart to copy the feeling.

"You won't," I replied quickly, forcing a hopeful tone, even though it sounded more fake than anything else.

He did not respond, only hugged me tighter, unable to let go. So I pulled him further onto me, forcing our bodies to move until my back reached the headboard, Rhylan resting on top of my shaky legs. I didn't mind the weight. At this point my entire body had been blown away by him and I had no control left over my muscles.

I kept quiet and listened to his breathing, followed as his lungs inhaled and released the air and my hands caressed every single part of him that I could reach.

I did not know what time it was when his breathing evened, head still basking in the warmth of my chest, his body completely relaxing and falling prey to sleep just as the first waves of dawn started painting the sky.

At the sound of my voice, Rhy's eyes opened, gazing around the room and out the window at the lit sky.

"Shhh, you're okay," I murmured again and reached for his cheek, fingers caressing his tight jaw.

"I'm sorry, I didn't mean to fall asleep, didn't want to waste time," he started shaking his head in disbelief and I stopped him with a soft kiss.

"You needed the rest. And god knows I couldn't take it anymore," I both giggled and blushed at everything that happened the night before. Our wedding night.

I suddenly remembered the box on the nightstand, which had been delivered only an hour ago via the miraculous ways of Mark, whom I had gotten myself acquainted with, while Rhy rested.

"A wedding gift," I announced proudly and offered the black velvet box, tied with a black silk ribbon, of course.

He remained silent for a split second, taking me in, then quickly shifted from the covers and reached for the box, unsure.

"I love presents," he admitted with excitement and shattered the ribbon in an abrupt motion, ripping parts of the box as he did so, to find my present. "What is it made of?" Rhy removed the bracelet from the box and my worries quickly went away.

I had texted Mark and asked him to find a black tourmaline bracelet. I worried it would be beady and weird looking. Instead, what the marvellous hacker had brought was a stunning and elegant piece of jewellery, made entirely from the crystal, each piece sculpted and shaped to look like watch chains, all connecting in harmony to make a stunning, and very manly piece of jewellery.

"It's black tourmaline," I announced as he observed the elegant design. "I researched it but I'm not sure if it's right or not. It's one of the stones that helps travelling between the worlds. Makes it easier," I explained.

Rhy's eyes darted to me and I read pure love in them. He couldn't say the words, but he nodded once, showing how grateful he was, then extended his left wrist to me along with the piece of jewellery to help him stretch it along his wrist.

"Now you can find your way to your wife quicker," I forced a smile and planted a kiss on the palm of his hand, which he immediately closed after my lips abandoned the area, sealing the kiss in.

"I will," Rhy's features became sharp, haunted. "I swear it. I will return for you."

I was about to cry, so I shifted my head to the side and blinked the tears away. Unfortunately, the gesture was not too subtle or effective, because in the next instant, Rhy's arms were pulling me gently for another embrace.

I eagerly responded and wrapped my arms tightly around him, smelling his skin and basking in his touch, trying to hold onto him for as long as I could. To be able to remember the feeling of him while he was away.

We would have stayed like that for long minutes, both of us planting a kiss now and then on our partner's shoulder, neck, hair, lips. I knew he would not let go, not until I was ready to. I was also aware of the time difference and the fact that Anwen must be freaking out already waiting for him and I did not want to prolong her suffering. She would see Ansgar today, and knowing the need to be in a lover's arms, feeling it right that second, I could not delay their reunion any longer.

"We should get going," I announced and tried to detach myself from him. Rhy's muscles went tight for a mere moment, before I felt him nod and finally, let go.

"Okay," he murmured, barely audible. "There's extra clothes in the wardrobe," he announced and swallowed a dry lump, threatening to make his voice break.

"Thank you," I barely murmured as well and headed to the dresser. I did not waste time on make-up or hair. Today would be a terrible day and we both knew it. Plus he was my husband now, so he was entitled to see me at my worst.

I returned to the room to find Rhy looking as splendid as he always did, tapping on his phone. When he spotted me, he announced, "Mark is doing the final arrangements and you should get all the documents in the next couple of days. He also has your number, and will be at your service from today. So anything you need, text him and it will be done."

I frowned, not understanding what all this meant. What documents?

"If you want to visit your house again, text him and he'll send a security team with you, if you want to get rid of an appointment or anybody bothers you, he'll take care of things. Regarding the businesses, they are self-sufficient so you may get the odd email to confirm a purchase but it will be all already arranged."

"What businesses?" My husband frowned, as if it was the most obvious thing, yet I had no clue what he meant.

"Our businesses. They're yours too now. No need to worry, we have the right people in the right positions, so they take care of everything for us," he reassured me, a hand gently sliding down my arm.

"You are giving me access to your businesses? Billion dollar businesses?" I did not know if having so much sex drove him mad, but he sure looked like it.

Rhy said nothing, only reached for my hand and raised it to his mouth, planting a soft kiss on each of my fingertips. "And I will return to you. As soon as I am able."

His gaze darted to mine and I instantly nodded, unable to speak. I didn't care about his companies, his money or his hacker buddy or everything else that Rhy was suddenly and without even asking, giving me. All I wanted was him. To be with him, in this hotel room until the end of time. Until I grew old and he would get sick of me, until we'd had so much sex that our bodies gave out and then we had to chill in bed and watch every movie in the history of mankind together.

This was too sudden, too abrupt, and my heart was breaking. How did I come to love him this much, so deeply in such a short time was beyond me. One thing I knew for sure, was that I would never be the same after Rhylan.

Whether he returned for me or not, he had completely and utterly changed me.

"Are you ready?" he asked, though we both knew the answer and none of us wanted to say it.

No. I will never be ready for this. I will never be able to let you go.

Instead, I nodded and wrapped my arms around his shoulders, closing my eyes for what was to come. Seconds later, we were in his room, at the Odstar home. Tears started flowing down my face and I was unable to control them. Unable to do anything but let them shed away pieces of my heart.

Rhy squeezed me tightly again. "I love you," he whispered, planting a gentle kiss on my cheek. We would not say goodbye, even though we hadn't decided it, we both instinctively followed the unspoken rule.

"I love you too," I responded and locked my lips with his, enjoying one final wet kiss, because my tears had decided just then, to never stop falling.

Still wrapped in his arms, we walked to Anwen's room,

where Rhy knocked gently to announce our arrival.

"Ready sprout?" His entire demeanour changed with those two words, becoming the dreadful faerie once more, adopting the role he cast himself into.

Only for me, I understood. Only for me he would be gentle and caring, sweet and charming, funny and ridiculous. My husband, I smiled to myself at the sight of him and felt pride. Pride for his strength and determination, for the power he had to face it all. I could do it, I told myself. I could do it too.

With my back straight and a breath of fresh air, I quickly hugged my friend, who was jumping up and down with excitement, and followed her down the stairs to bid her farewells to her parents.

"Take care Anwen, I'm sure we'll see each other soon," I repeated the same words I did upstairs and watched her practically fly out the main entrance door with excitement.

With a last glance that showed all the promise and love we had secretly shared, Rhy picked up the keys and headed out the door.

I remained frozen at the entrance, seeing Anwen happily waving goodbye while Rhy's voice echoed in my mind.

"I love you," he whispered one last time, before the car disappeared through the gates.

Day 56

"Okay, perfect Cressida, one more take just to make sure and we're done," the director announced and I plastered my seductive smile once again for the camera. We had been shooting the commercial for the past five hours and I'd stayed in front of the wind machine for so long that I had a permanent buzzing in my ears. The requirements of camera-perfect, I internally sighed as they started making the final count.

My feet blistered in the six-inch heels I had to walk in since we started shooting and I wouldn't be surprised to find blood when I took them out. The silicone cushion-pads I usually wore had shifted and made walking even more uncomfortable. I was ready to finish filming and knew that if we stopped even for a minute and I released my feet from their trap, they would swell so much I wouldn't be able to walk for the rest of the day.

So I took a deep breath in, found my character and started frolicking around the studio, wearing a short dress and an umbrella, walking as though the world belonged to me. And it was all due to the lipstick I had to remember to put on suddenly, just as I spotted a hot guy walking down the street. Who would, of course, instantly fall in love with me, and it was all due to that perfect shade of red.

"And, we're done," Yiryam, the director, announced and soon after, everyone started clapping. I smiled politely and bowed slowly, grateful for the applause and completion of a good day's work, especially because I was so excited to go home and go straight to bed.

As soon as all the photos, videos, tiktoks, insta lives and celebratory toasts were done, activities that took another two hours of me being in those dreadful heels, I went back to my changing room and threw the damned things on the floor. Whoever invented high heels and thought it was a good idea for women to wear them deserved to burn in hell. Slowly.

I got out of the costume and went straight to the shower cabin, allowing the hot steam to fall over my fancy hairdo and make-up, letting it all be washed away. I knew it wasn't the most inspired of ideas and I would come out looking like a dishevelled zombie, but I was tired and aching and could barely stand, so I wasn't particularly fussed about my appearance. It was a ride straight home, not that I spent too much time there in the past month, anyway.

I took every opportunity there was to travel. A lot. I had probably been in ten countries since Rhy and Anwen left and surrounded myself with so many people I had to sneakily take photos of them and add tags on my phone to remember their names. Even so, I felt more alone than ever, and I didn't have my best friend to talk to. Or my husband, whom I hadn't heard a single word from, even though he promised to return.

The times I did spend at the apartment were mostly late nights, when I arrived so tired that I threw myself in bed and fell instantly asleep, only to wake up in the morning and do it all over again.

I must have gotten home at around one and as usual, I found something to snack on from the fridge while I replied to some comments and tags on socials, a random movie keeping me company in the background before I fell asleep on the sofa.

A long series of beeping sounds woke me up and the strain in my neck forced a sharp pain to hit abruptly. I was sleeping so badly lately and always felt tired, no matter how many hours of rest I got in. I even started taking tablets to help me fall asleep quicker, but I was so jetlagged and had such a weird sleeping schedule that nothing seemed to work.

Ping after ping, my phone screamed for attention and I forced myself up, stretching my neck a couple of times before I found it in one of my fuzzy slippers.

Mark: Good morning, Mrs Thompson

Mark: I cancelled your interview with the shampoo brand tonight and scheduled a business meeting. I will email you the address shortly

Mark: Mrs Thompson, please can I have your confirmation

Mark: Mrs Thompson it is important, these are business partners Mr Gordon has invested years working with

Mark: Please confirm, I have resent the email.

The chain of messages showed a highly stressed Mark who kept messaging me every ten minutes on the hour. There must have been about thirty texts and I had slept through every single one. Details of a late evening dinner at a fancy restaurant which I had to attend?

It sounded overly strange, especially since in the past month, all I had to do was sign an initial series of documents that added my bank account to the billion dollar businesses, which I reluctantly did with very shaky hands, especially since I had absolutely no idea what I was doing.

After that I kept myself to myself, only with Mark messaging from time to time about several updates, until I asked him to set up an email notification rather than him having to message me account balances that had so many zeros I initially thought they were scam messages.

The fact that I suddenly had to attend a business dinner at one of the fanciest locations in the city, when I had absolutely no idea about what said businesses were, felt like a complete lunacy to me. I quickly grabbed my phone and started texting back. Strangely, even though we'd been in contact a few times, Mark and I never spoke on the phone. I had no idea who he was, or where he was, or if he even was a he.

Me: Sorry, I was asleep, long day yesterday

Me: I am not ignoring you, I promise, I didn't hear my phone

Me: Is there no one else to cover this?

Mark: Mrs Thompson, it is your business and the new partners want to meet the owner.

Me: Nope, it's Rhy's business and I have no clue what to do. Isn't there a CEO that can cover this?

Mark's reply was a screenshot of the business listing, containing name, business number, office location and CEO: Cressida Thompson.

Me: You know I didn't read that mountain of documents you send me to sign

Mark: I didn't expect you to, Mrs Thompson, it was all already taken care of

Me: What do I even do? What should I say?

Mark: Even though it is a business meeting, it is not business related. Treat it like you would any other meeting, where you introduce the partners before signing a contract.

Me: I spent all day in high heels yesterday and my ankles are screaming in pain. I hate this

Mark: Please confirm your attendance

Me: Fiiiiiine

As encouragement from the caring neighbourhood hacker, an hour later a bag of feet-goodies was delivered to my door, which included several creams and blister patches, a set of comfy heel soles, bath salts and novocaine spray.

At nine o'clock sharp I was dressed, hair done, make-up perfectly arranged, wearing a satin low-cut open back dress and, once more, six inch high heels. I made an effort to look absolutely stunning, the ombre effect on the dress perfectly matching my clutch and shoes.

If I couldn't speak business to these people, I might as well make an appearance and waste half an hour on compliments and casual talk about brands, designers and shoes. I could at least do that. I would not disappoint Rhy and make him lose this, because if Mark had sent me there, it must have been for a good reason.

A black limo already waited for me outside, so I greeted the driver and jumped in, helping myself to a glass of champagne, to banish some of the nerves. I didn't know if it was necessary or not, so I texted Mark to let him know I was on my way, to which he instantly replied with a single word. "Enjoy"

I wasn't really sure what I was supposed to be enjoying, apart from looking stunning and the amazing champagne I had a second serving of before we arrived, but fine, I'll take it. I'll try to enjoy it.

As soon as we arrived, the driver jumped from his seat and hurried to open the door for me. Not only that, he insisted on escorting me to the entrance door and when I arrived he unbuttoned his jacket to pop out a single yellow rose, which he handed to me with a slight bow. I smiled and thanked him, and he too wished me a pleasant evening before he left me with the host, who also had a yellow rose for me.

"Mrs Thompson, we are so delighted to welcome you tonight. Please follow me." With that, he turned and offered me his arm. Weird, but okay. I grabbed it and let myself be led by the man.

We took a few steps to a mirrored set of doors which instantly opened, revealing a line of people, whom I guessed were the waiters, forming a pathway towards another set of doors, each holding a bouquet of yellow roses.

What in the hell?

I bowed my head slowly at the people gathered along the way, trying to greet or at least look at each and every one and when we were halfway through the corridor, I asked if the others had already arrived, imagining the awkwardness of this host greeting every single one of them the same way.

He nodded again and responded with a smile. "Yes ma'am, he has been anxiously waiting for you."

"*He* has? Who has?" I frowned at the man and then it clicked. Mark, the sudden urgent meeting, the limo, champagne and yellow roses.

"Rhy?"

I barely breathed and losing all control of myself and my actions, I let go of the man's arm and started running towards the double doors, which immediately opened into a ballroom.

A ballroom, filled with chandeliers, candles and tons of yellow roses, petals even falling from the ceiling. I looked around me, surprised and confused, hoping, hoping that he was truly here.

Suddenly an orchestra started playing and I turned to my left, following the sound. I hadn't even noticed them, surrounded by all the roses. And they were playing Rose's theme song from Titanic. Oh god, I wanted to faint. This was perfect, more than perfect, so amazing that I couldn't even think of such a scene in my wildest dreams.

"We never had a wedding dance." His voice was a whisper, wrapping around the song and as soon as I felt it my entire body shattered, goose bumps adorning the entirety of my skin while my heart started drumming like crazy. I turned to find him looking stunning as always, towering over me, those onyx eyes pierced on mine, that sly smirk on his face.

"Rhy—" I barely murmured and threw myself in his arms. The next moment I was flying in the air and he spun me around, the weight of my body meaningless for him.

"My love," he replied, eyes gleaming with joy before he placed his lips on mine, kissing me with passion and rage, with desire and longing. How I missed the feel of him, the taste of him, the smell of mint and spice he always left across the room.

We held each other for long minutes, kissing and caressing, swaying slowly to the rhythm of the music, unable to let go, unable to stop kissing and touching, the proof that we were finally together.

"I missed you so much," I finally spoke, cupping his face and slowly caressing his jaw.

Rhy returned my smile and closed the embrace, pinning my chest to his.

"And I missed you, my love. So much."

We kissed again, and again, and again, until the musicians probably got fed up with playing, but I did not care, could not pay attention to anything or anyone that wasn't him. Because he had returned. Just as he promised.

"Is Anwen okay?" I instantly asked, and Rhy nodded, confirming with a smile. "She knows, and I am free."

"You have to tell me all about it," I asked, even though I was aware it would prove complicated for him to find the time to speak when my tongue kept dancing with his own.

"I will, sunshine. I will share it all with you," Rhy agreed, squeezing me tighter and spinning me once again in the air before he gently placed my feet back on the ground. "But first, I have an important question for you."

My eyes widened, gripping his shoulders to ground myself into this dream. "What is it?"

"Would you like to be my queen?"

Follow Cressida and Rhylan's story in
Tales of Wind and Storm

XANDRA NOEL

For a new author, reviews are everything, so if you enjoyed this book, please give it some stars!

More from the author

Discover the Tales of Earth and Leaves series
Tales of Earth and Leaves
Tales of Fire and Embers
Tales of Wind and Storm

Discover *Love, Will, an LGBT historical fiction*

If you enjoyed this book, you'll love the FREE bonus story *Tales of War and Fire.* Subscribe to Xandra's newsletter and get your copy, along with bonus chapters and fun content.

www. xandranoel.com

Thank you for choosing to have a read!

Printed in Poland
by Amazon Fulfillment
Poland Sp. z o.o., Wrocław